Y0-AGU-553

Lazy Fascist Press
an imprint of Eraserhead Press
PO Box 10065
Portland, OR 97296

www.lazyfascistpress.com

ISBN: 978-1-62105-157-2

Edited by Kirsten Alene

Cover Design by Matthew Revert
www.matthewrevert.com

Interior Illustrations by Alan M. Clark

Printed in the USA.

Say Anything But Your Prayers

Alan M. Clark

A Lazy Fascist Original Novel

FOREWORD

This is a work of fiction inspired by the life of Elizabeth Stride, a woman believed to be the third victim of Jack the Ripper. For purposes of storytelling, I have not adhered strictly to her history. I have assigned to my main character emotional characteristics and reactions that seem consistent with her life and circumstances. I've addressed puzzling events in Elizabeth Stride's life, and a mysterious confusion that occurred during the coroner's inquest into her murder concerning her identity.

To be clear, this novel is not about Jack the Ripper. The series itself is not about the killer. Instead, each novel in the series explores the life of a different victim.

I wrote this note in the month of October, a time for scary fun. I truly enjoy the cute horror of Halloween and a good, over-the-top zombie film, yet as one who has always been intrigued by the dark and disturbing, as a practitioner in the horror genre, a professional writer for almost two decades, and an illustrator for almost three, sometimes that sort of fun scare falls flat. My interest has been drawn over time to the real horror of history and the lessons to be learned from it.

Long ago, when I first learned of Jack the Ripper and the murders associated with the killer, I was, as most everyone is, intrigued by the endless speculation about who he might have been (I use male pronouns when referring to him merely because of the name Jack; though we don't know the gender of the Whitechapel Murderer). The more I read about the murders and the various theories, the less interested I was in the killer and the more intrigued I became with the environment in which the murders took place. As I learned more about Victorian London and how rapidly it changed due to the Industrial Revolution, the more interesting I found the lives of those who lived there at the time. Although I couldn't learn much about the killer, I could gain some knowledge of the five female victims. Potentially, there are more than five, but those considered canonical victims are Mary Ann Nichols, Annie Chapman, Elizabeth Stride, Catherine Eddowes, and Mary Jane Kelly.

Coroner's inquests were held to determine the cause of death for each of the women. The inquiries are essentially trials, with juries and witnesses to help make a determination about the manner of a victim's demise. The verdict in each of the five cases was "Wilful murder against some person or persons unknown."

The words, actions, movements, and motivations of each of the women are most clearly known to history closest to the time of their deaths because of the testimony of the witnesses called during the inquests. In some cases, such as that of Elizabeth Stride, the last couple of hours were recounted in detail, and in other cases, such as that of Catherine Eddowes, we have a good idea what she did within several days of her death. The farther we go into the past away from the hour of their deaths, however, the less detailed and the more generalized is the information about them. Within the few years prior to their deaths, all five had suffered real hardship—all had engaged in prostitution to survive, most, if not all, had been active alcoholics, and most had spent time in the dehumanizing workhouse system.

In Victorian England, the Industrial Revolution had led to large-scale unemployment, much the way the Tech Revolution has done in America today. Victorian London, much like large American cities today, suffered from overcrowding and large numbers of homeless.

We can see a modern reflection of the victims of Jack the Ripper in the homeless of twenty-first century America. Much of the cause of that homelessness went unseen in Victorian times, as it does now. With the rise in the numbers of the homeless, then as now, people had a tendency to shy away from the problem.

My natural inclination is to avoid knowing why so many people are hungry and without shelter. I want to look away, and I don't want to look away. My experience is that many people are just as ambivalent. Many of the homeless are intoxicated much of the time or begging for the means to become intoxicated. I can easily become disgusted with the endless need of the addicts among the homeless. I could justify my righteousness by blaming their lack of hygiene, and their crimes of desperation. However, I am a sober alcoholic and expect myself to have compassion for them, even when it doesn't come naturally. There, but for providence, go I.

Although I avoid those who are clearly intoxicated, on occasion I've asked someone begging on the street for their story. Most aren't good at telling a story, perhaps because they are rarely asked to tell one. Even so, from what they say, I always get the sense that they have had happier times, that they have capabilities, and that they have aspirations involving their own personal interests and those whom they love.

Worse than the surface irritation of having to deal with a person who might be slovenly, dirty, inconvenient, or in-my-face is the emotional stress of considering the plight of an unfortunate person. My immediate response is to want to look away. I speak of my experience to take responsibility for my reactions, yet I'm not alone. We find it easy to scorn the beggars on the streets and then project that disdain on all homeless people, further isolating them. As a result, the down and out are less likely to find help when in danger. If they are seriously harmed or killed, fewer people step forward to try to find out what happened. Those who prey upon the homeless more easily get away with their crimes. The same was true for the down and out of Victorian London.

What events in the lives of the five Jack the Ripper victims led to their demise on the streets of London? How much of the way they lived was a result of the choices they made? What was beyond their control? Were they chosen at random by their killer, or did he choose them because he knew that fewer people would step forward to find out what happened to them? We don't have good, solid answers to these questions.

My impression is that their choices had something to do with securing their wellbeing, however, much of their existence was beyond their control. The environment of London itself was a danger. Literally hundreds of thousands of Londoners were killed by the pollution in the air, water, and food. New industries popped up everywhere to support the burgeoning population and to exploit the cheap labor market. Small factories occupied converted tenements or houses that once held families in residential neighborhoods. Sometimes, only a part of such a tenement or house was occupied by industry while the rest still functioned as a residence for individuals or families. With an increase in the use of chemistry, and with little knowledge of the damage many chemicals inflicted upon the bodies of those exposed to them, industries, such as matchmaking, destroyed the lives of their workers and those living within close proximity to production. Those who suffered often did so without knowing why until it was too late. Matchmaking is only one example of the industrial poisoning of Londoners. Deadly chemicals were everywhere. They were used in medicines and in prepared foods as preservatives. Madness abounded, if not as a result of the emotional hardships of life, then from chemical damage to the brain.

A life of poverty in London was slowly killing all of the Ripper's victims. Survival within that environment is the story that intrigues me. Those are lives I can relate to because I see parallels with life in my own time.

Regardless of whether the Ripper's victims had few opportunities to live better lives or were responsible in large part for their predicaments, their legacy is pitiful and poignant. Not the cute horror of Halloween perhaps or the over-the-top-turned-almost-cartoon horror of slasher and zombie films, the stories of the five women are full of emotional content, conflict, and drama. What happened to the victims of Jack the Ripper is *true* horror, and in the telling of those tales we are reminded that the more things change, the more they stay the same.

When I was growing up, my mother had a strange way of watching scary movies on television with the family; she'd stand in the hallway beside the living-room, peeking around the corner at the TV, ready to run away if the film became too scary. Is that the way we as a society treat true horror? We all love a fun scare, but when the suffering becomes too real, we want to run away because it's painful to witness. I suppose I'm saying that if fewer of us looked away, if we had the courage to see, there might be less actual horror in the world. So here's to remaining in the living-room of life with our eyes wide open.

And so to the life of Elizabeth Stride...

—Alan M. Clark
Eugene, Oregon

Say Anything But Your Prayers

1

THE PURSUIT OF SOMETHING BETTER

Whitechapel, London, September 30, 1888

Chilled from standing on Berner Street in the damp night, watching for her client's return, Elizabeth cursed herself silently, and decided that if the fellow didn't come back by the time she finished her grapes, she'd give up on him.

She had met the gentleman on Aldgate High Street and they'd spent a couple of hours together, eating and drinking at the Bricklayer's Arms pub a short distance away, and then walking to Berner Street. All the while, they'd talked, laughed, and paused occasionally for a bit of canoodling. He was a square-built man, old enough to be established but young enough to have kept his looks. His accent was odd, perhaps American. In his dark suit, overcoat, and billycock, he appeared to be a man of business, not a laborer.

The gentleman bought her black grapes at Packer's greengrocer down the lane. Although pleased with the gift, Elizabeth had to be careful with grapes since all except the juice of the fruit gave her a stomach ache. She rolled one grape around in her mouth to extract its nectar, while he ate a handful of them.

The fruit was an extravagance that suggested he was a generous and imaginative fellow who quite possibly saw their time together as more than merely a transaction. Indeed, she and the gentleman were getting along so well, she'd begun to think he might be the one who would take her away from the East End and provide for her in years to come. Elizabeth had been looking for something better throughout her life; a better home, better health, better employment, better food, better friends, and, of course, a better man.

Before her husband, Jon, died, he had advised her to find another man to take care of her. She had been with her cash carrier, Mr. Kidney, for several years now, and though she had sexual relations with him, he was a ponce. Almost any situation would be better than what she had with him.

Elizabeth was trying to think of a way to draw her client closer, to encourage his tendency to treat her as a lover, when he'd given her a big smile, and said, "You hold here. I'll go to my room and be back in a trice with a bottle of fine, sweet wine."

"You could get a bottle at The Nelson, there on the corner," she said, pointing.

"Not like the bottle I've got in my room."

Elizabeth didn't want him to get away. "I'll go with you."

He looked down, shaking his head slowly, and she knew he didn't want to be seen entering his home with a woman of her caliber. "It's not far," he said, looking up again. "I'll be right back with the sweetest wine you've ever tasted."

Elizabeth had a craving for sweets and was inclined to risk separation from her client to have some of the wine. She also needed to spit out the grape skin, seeds, and pulp, and not wanting to be indelicate in his presence, she had merely nodded her head.

Bloody Hell, I should have got his name before he walked away!

Currently, the dampness from the scattered rains were bringing out the ache in her old injury. Elizabeth bent and rubbed the unevenness of her right shin, where the bones had not been set correctly after her fall in the barn thirty-five years earlier. A drink would help ease the pain, and she thought about going into The Nelson and trying to find a fellow to buy her one. No, she might miss her client's return.

She ate her grapes slowly. Seven remained in the sack she held in her left hand. One stem of the fruit lay on the wet footway at her feet. As she wiped grape juice from her lips with one of her handkerchiefs, Elizabeth peered into the gloom, looking out for her client among the people moving about the area. Although after midnight, the neighborhood was remarkably busy. She was nearsighted, and, despite the numerous street lamps, people walking along the lane were almost upon her by the time she saw them clearly. Accustomed to the risks of waiting alone on the street, she restrained her unease. For good or ill, she had the voices of her two selves to keep her company; Bess, the callow child of hope, and Liza, the cynical, hardbitten opportunist.

2

FAVORITES

Hisingen, Torslanda, Sweden, mid-summer 1855

Elizabeth's mother, Fru Beata Carlsdotter, was clearly in a mood. Placing a breakfast of bread and butter on the kitchen table before her daughter, she said, "Foolish girl."

"How many times must you say that, Mother?" Elizabeth asked.

"Every time I have to do for you what you cannot with a cast on your leg." Fru Carlsdotter pushed a dark curl of hair away from her green eyes, wiped sweat from her plump face, and turned away to clean pots and pans.

Elizabeth was tired of being reminded of her mistake, and she was irritable for her own reasons. Something had changed in her outlook since the accident. A darker voice emerged from her thoughts. Sometimes the thoughts themselves did not seem to be the notions of a twelve-year-old. She wasn't sure she liked the new facet of her temperament.

She wanted vodka.

A loud rap came from the corner of the room. One of Elizabeth's crutches had fallen to the floor. Fru Carlsdotter dried her hands and moved to the corner. Struggling against her own plump belly, she bent slowly to pick up the crutch. She leaned it into the corner with the other one. "Foolish girl," she said.

"Mother!"

As Fru Carlsdotter turned back to her work, tears threatened to spill from her eyes. She wiped her face quickly.

"Why are you crying?" Elizabeth asked without sympathy.

"Your father wants Kristina to leave home. I suppose I should thank you. Your sister was to go to Gothenburg today to apply for her change of address certificate, but instead she works with your father, doing *your* work. She'll be home a little longer."

Elizabeth might have guessed the sadness had something to do with Kristina. Their father, Herr Gustav Ericsson, was a hard man used to having his way. Her older sister, beautiful blonde and blue-eyed Kristina, currently seventeen years old, had refused to marry any of the three young men who had asked for her hand. All three were men of her father's choosing. Herr Ericsson, disgusted with Kristina's unwillingness, had put his foot down. "If you're not wed by the end of spring," he'd said last autumn, "you'll be going into the city to look for work. The farm can't continue to support us all." Summer had come and Kristina remained unwed, while the price of milk, butter, and potatoes continued to fall.

Kristina didn't want to leave home. Elizabeth couldn't understand her sister's desire to stay. Life on the farm was monotonous, full of hard work with little social contact. Elizabeth yearned for something better, to be away from her family, to start a new life with an opportunity for adventure. She looked forward to a time when she would be old enough and smart enough to find her own way.

Elizabeth heard her father come in through the front door.

As he passed by on his way out the back door, Herr Ericsson glanced into the kitchen. He was tall and thin, with a dour face framed by graying brown hair and whiskers. He didn't smile for her. The only time he seemed happy with her was when she made his morning coffee and brought it to him. She hadn't been able to do that since breaking her leg. Being the only one within the household who could consistently make a good cup of coffee was a point of pride for Elizabeth. The trick was getting the cast iron roaster heated properly in the fireplace coals before putting the beans in it. The grinding and boiling was much easier to get right. Even her mother, who was quite good in the kitchen, couldn't seem to make good coffee. Once Elizabeth left home, Herr Ericsson would surely miss her every time he wanted a cup.

"I'm certain you will not cry for *me* when *I* leave home," she said. She was surprised at her bitter words. They seemed to come from the new unnamed voice within her thoughts.

Fru Carlsdotter spun around and glared, her face reddening and her hand raised to strike. "If not for your injury, Liza Black Tongue, I would slap your mouth."

Elizabeth cringed.

Fru Carlsdotter had lowered her hand, and turned away to clean up the kitchen. "You have been lashing out with that tongue ever since you broke your leg, *foolish* girl."

Normally, Fru Carlsdotter called Elizabeth Liza Black Tongue when she was caught in a lie. Lately, however, her mother also used the named when Elizabeth spoke angrily.

Since breaking her leg, Elizabeth had been unaccountably disagreeable with her mother. Kristina was Fru Carlsdotter's expressed favorite child, and had always received preferential treatment, but Elizabeth had never before shown resentment regarding that.

Even as she tried to dismiss her spiteful attitude as unworthy childishness, the new voice within her thoughts said, *She would send you away now if she could keep her precious Kristina.* The bitterness of the voice surprised her; so much so that the words she'd heard in her head seemed to have come from someone else.

Ever since she could remember, she'd thought of herself as Bess, after her early childhood mispronunciation of her name as Elizabess. Bess was an innocent, one trusting of others and frequently anticipating only the best. She was gullible, and always seeking approval. She rarely spoke with bitterness. The new voice was different; mistrustful of others, even her parents.

But, then, Elizabeth *was* different since the injury. She had been tricked by the oldest of her two younger brothers, Caspar, on the day she fell in the barn.

"The beam is only fifteen feet above the floor," he'd said. "Mother says you're light as a feather, so, if you tumble, the hay will break your fall."

If Fru Carlsdotter had said that she was light as a feather, that was a rare expression of approval. She usually reserved her praise for Kristina alone.

Their father had warned against jumping from the loft into piles of hay much higher than the one to which Caspar referred. Herr Ericsson had forbidden the children to walk out on the beam from which depended pulley blocks, hooks and ropes. Father had said there might be tools hidden beneath the hay that could seriously harm a falling child. But Elizabeth knew there were no tools beneath the hay on that day. She had no intention of falling, and she liked the idea of proving her mother right. Nimbly traversing the beam that ran across the open space between the loft and the splintery wall would be demonstration enough. If she slipped, the consequences could not be *too* severe.

Caspar's mischief was not unusual. Elizabeth might fault him for trying to trick her, but knew he wasn't to blame for what happened. Although she'd wanted to believe otherwise, she had known that walking on the beam in the barn was dangerous.

Elizabeth had started out across the dusty timber like a music box ballerina, humming a ballad from a broadside her father had brought home from a visit to Gothenburg, taking mincing, delicate steps over the draped lengths of rope and the metal fasteners of the tackle, her arms outstretched. She felt beautiful in her light green morning shift and undergarments, was exhilarated by the view from the height and by the risk. Elizabeth would have willingly suffered her father's punishment if only her mother could see her.

Her left foot hung under one of the loops of rope and she teetered toward the left. A sudden rush of energy made her skin feel tight. Too late, she bent to her right and thrust out her arms in that direction to compensate. Even so, she believed she'd checked her fall, and grinned uneasily. But as she fell past the beam, her smile fled and she gulped a breath to scream. Striking the floor with a loud snap in her shin, the scream was forced from her lungs along with her breath. Elizabeth lay stunned, an odd numbness in her lower right leg.

Caspar was above her making a fuss, his eyes wide and his mouth working, but she couldn't understand him.

Elizabeth tried to rise, and the pain struck her. She saw the lower portion of her right leg and foot lying at an odd angle, and her voice returned along with her scream.

Caspar put his hands to his ears and ran from the barn. He returned shortly with their younger brother Sveinn and their father. Mercifully, Elizabeth wasn't aware of much for a time until she found herself on the kitchen table. Her mother and Sveinn were bracing her upper body and Caspar held her left leg down while her father worked to set her broken limb. The pain was excruciating as he pulled and twisted the lower portion of her leg, trying to position the ends of the break together. Elizabeth cried out for him to stop.

He was clearly frustrated as he worked. Was his frustration with her? Was he so angry with her for walking on the beam that he would punish her by making the setting of her break more painful? He looked at her with a grimace, and made one last effort to twist her shin. The pressure on her leg was so painful, Elizabeth wrenched her left leg free of Caspar's grip and kicked her father in the face. Blood sprayed from Herr Ericsson's nose and he backed away, cursing.

Elizabeth screamed with the pain. She couldn't catch her breath, and her vision darkened. With that, the pain lessened. She gulped for more breath and gratefully moved toward the darkness.

The last thing she heard before she slept was her father's voice, saying, "That's the best I can do."

She awoke with her leg splinted and covered with starched bandages. The pain was nearly unbearable. Fru Carlsdotter fed her vodka to ease the pain. Herr Ericsson avoided looking at her most of the time, and when he did, his gaze wasn't a kindly one. His nose was swollen and blue.

Eventually a doctor came to the house and examined Elizabeth.

"The break was not set perfectly, but it will have to do," he said. He put a proper plaster cast on it.

Your father has left you a cripple, Elizabeth heard herself thinking. Cold and bitter, the thoughts sounded out of place in her head at the time. That cynical voice of caution—so distinctly different from the naive child, Bess, she'd always heard before—had been with her since her fall, its presence growing steadily stronger.

As she toyed with her buttered bread and watched her mother clean the kitchen, the new voice gave her a bit of advice. *Your brother tricked you because you trusted him. A mistrustful nature will help to protect you.*

That is Liza Black Tongue speaking, Elizabeth told herself, and she wondered if she should listen. For a twelve-year-old with little worldly experience, the message seemed to be good advice, yet she hesitated to encourage the cynical facet of herself. She wasn't sure she liked Liza.

Fru Carlsdotter was slamming pots and pans around, a sure

sign of her irritation with Elizabeth.

You'd better be good or she will have your father send you *away soon*, Liza warned.

She's right, Elizabeth thought.

Possibly, Liza had her uses.

"I'm sorry, Mother," Elizabeth said. "The ache in my leg makes me irritable."

"It's been two months, now," her mother said without turning. "That excuse has worn thin."

Make her feel sorry for you, Liza said. *Tell her a lie if you have to.*

Elizabeth didn't want to tell a fib. Still, if she must be mistrustful of others, there was no reason she should remain trustworthy. "A beetle crawled into my cast last night while I was in bed, and chewed my leg. When it crawled out this morning, I smashed it."

Fru Carlsdotter set down the cleaning rag she'd been using and turned, a skeptical look on her face.

Elizabeth donned her most innocent Bess expression and gave her mother an even gaze. "The itch of it kept me from sleep, and you know the break hurts most when I'm weary."

Fru Carlsdotter looked troubled for a moment, then said, "Perhaps you need a bit of vodka and a nap."

Elizabeth had to control herself to keep from showing her delight. She hadn't had vodka for over a week. Although she didn't need the intoxicant for pain, she had been craving it, and didn't want her mother to see her eagerness.

Yes, Elizabeth decided, she did like Liza, after all.

3

A NEW LIFE

Fru Carlsdotter did cry when Elizabeth left home at seventeen years of age.

Elizabeth had not expected to weep. She was happy to be leaving. She had responded no better than her sister had to the very same men presented by her father as suitors. Like her father, they were farmers. She'd seen enough of that sort to prefer taking a chance on making a life in the city. Elizabeth wanted something better, and would make a new start in Gothenburg where she hoped to find a little adventure.

Fru Carlsdotter took the morning off from her job as a maid, risking dismissal to be home to see Elizabeth off. Her father and two brothers, however, seemed to begrudge her the farewell during their busy work day.

Elizabeth was to walk to the farm south of her home to ride into the city with the Adamsson family in their wagon. When the time came for her to turn away from her mother and begin walking, she could not stop her tears.

As her sister had done, Elizabeth would live for a time in Gothenburg with an old friend of her mother's family, Hortense Andersdotter. Elizabeth had met the woman once many years ago, but didn't remember her well. She knew that Fru Andersdotter was in her eighty-first year, and that she'd suffered a recent decline in health.

In early September 1860, Elizabeth arrived at Fru Andersdotter's small wooden house in the Majorna district in Ösp Lane, and rang the bell at the gate that led into a neglected garden in front. The woman who emerged from the house and slowly made her way across the garden was withered and stooped. Halfway to the gate, she seemed to focus on Elizabeth and motioned for her to enter.

Elizabeth passed through the gate cautiously and approached. Fru Andersdotter had lost most of her hair. She was dressed in stained nightclothes. Although her wrinkled face was severe, her features took on a warm expression when she got a good look at Elizabeth.

"Fru Andersdotter," Elizabeth said.

"Please call me Hortense," the old woman said, smiling. "I'm glad you've come. You look so like your mother."

Elizabeth didn't know if she'd be comfortable using the old woman's first name. She set her bags down on the path. The late summer sun felt good on her face. "You got my letter, then."

"Yes, but I have not found anyone to help me write back to you yet." Hortense held up her twisted, arthritic hands. "I can no longer write."

"I took the chance of coming—"

"Yes, you needn't apologize," the old woman said, her smile growing larger. "If you will cook and clean, just as your sister did, you may stay with me."

Elizabeth smiled and nodded eagerly.

"What a relief," Hortense said in a giddy voice. "I will live longer if I don't have to depend on my neighbor to feed me."

"Is she that bad of a cook?" Elizabeth asked.

Hortense took Elizabeth's hands and squeezed them gently. "No, but like everything else, it costs money for her to prepare my food. The roof over my head and the meals I eat are paid for by what little remains of my dear, departed Herr Bjorkman's estate."

Elizabeth tilted her head, a question in her eyes.

"My husband," Hortense said, answering the unspoken question. "He did not prepare for me to live so long. The funds will run out soon. I hope to join him before that happens."

Elizabeth hid her surprise at such frank language. Still, she thought she liked the old woman.

Hortense released her. Elizabeth picked up her bags and followed the woman into the house. She was greeted by a powerful stench. Moving through the interior, she identified the sources of the smell: unwashed clothing, a dirty kitchen, and a multitude of vessels serving as makeshift chamber pots, all filled with slops. Her eyes went wide. She realized her mouth had dropped open and closed it quickly to help keep out the smell and the flies that buzzed all around.

"I often cannot make it to the privy in time," Hortense said uncomfortably.

Elizabeth gave her a tight smile. "I'll get to work."

Elizabeth had the house cleaned up in two days. She couldn't get all of the smell out. Eventually, she grew accustomed to the odor, and couldn't smell it anymore.

She got along well with Hortense, but found herself devoting all her time to doing those things the old woman could not do for herself. Elizabeth thought back to the healing of her broken leg and how irritable her mother had been during that time. She understood and sympathized with Fru Carlsdotter's frustration.

To keep the house free of foul odor and flies, Elizabeth tried to support Hortense as she made her way to the privy behind the house. The old woman so often evacuated her bodily waste on the way, however, Elizabeth gave up on that form of assistance and turned to more frequent cleaning of chamber pots. Hortense owned two chamber pots, one for each of the house's bedrooms. So predictable had become unexpected loss of bowel control that Elizabeth kept in service two of the makeshift chamber pots, a large dented kettle and a crockery mixing bowl, so there would be one in each room of the house.

Although the food she prepared was spare, she was accustomed to eating little. She read to Hortense in the evening and remained dutifully by her side.

Elizabeth wrote to her sister, at the address their mother had provided, telling of her situation and expressing a desire to see her. At first she got no reply from Kristina. She kept writing, and, after a few weeks, a letter came.

Dearest Elizabeth,

Please forgive me for the delay in writing to you, but my life is too full for correspondence. With the children, I have too many responsibilities at this time to visit with you. I hope you find a good home in the city.

Please write again next year.

Most heartfelt regards,
Fru Kristina Gustavsdotter

Elizabeth had no desire to write to her sister again.

She became quite restless and bored, and wanted to leave Hortense to find a new home, yet she couldn't bring herself to abandon the old woman who so obviously needed help.

If you're more diligent in your care, Fru Andersdotter will recover her health, Bess said.

The old wretch is beyond help, Liza said. *Still, she might have money tucked away that she'll give you if you're a good enough companion.*

Elizabeth didn't believe either suggestion, and could see no way out. She had no time to look for a proper job, and she knew she would not feel good about herself if she left Hortense in the unfortunate position in which she'd found her. Apparently the old woman had no family to help out.

By mid-October, Hortense had noticed Elizabeth's restlessness. "You need to leave the house and see something of the city."

"I go to market for our food," Elizabeth said.

"Going to market and back is not enough. You should go out and have a good meal. I would go with you myself, but I fear I might not return. There's a nice young man who helped me one afternoon when I fell in the garden. I believe his name is Herr Lydersson. Klaudio is his given name, if I remember. He lives with his uncle in the green house across the lane. You're a pretty girl. If you spent time in the garden—"

"—And perhaps fell," Elizabeth said with a laugh. "I believe I've seen him—a handsome blonde fellow?"

"Yes," Hortense had a mischievous look in her eye. "Look out for him when you leave and return from market. You might like him."

The old woman's suggestion surprised Elizabeth—a young woman her age should have a chaperone for an outing with a young man.

She trusts you, Bess said. *You're mature for your age. She must trust the young man too.*

Although Elizabeth blamed Hortense's doddering mind for the neglect of propriety, she liked what Bess suggested. Elizabeth was currently responsible for herself, after all, since the old woman represented no reasonable adult protection.

In October, Elizabeth met Herr Lydersson much the way Hortense had suggested. He was perhaps twenty-five years old, of medium height and build, with a prominent nose, square, clean-shaved jaw, blue eyes, and light blonde hair worn a little long. They'd struck up a conversation in the lane between the houses. He'd asked Elizabeth to call him Klaudio, then invited her to have a meal with him at The Siren's Promise, a local tavern.

She accepted the invitation, prepared Hortense's dinner early, and walked with Klaudio about a quarter of a mile to the tavern.

"I work the docks for now," Klaudio said as they began their meal of herring, potatoes and vodka, "but will sail for England when I've saved a bit of money. My mother is English. When my father died a few years ago, she returned to her family there. Everything in London is bigger and better. I visited as a child, and saw the Great Exhibition at the Crystal Palace. Soon I'll return to England and build a new life."

Klaudio continued talking about England for some time, allowing for no interruption.

He's not interested in anything you have to say, Liza said. *He's up to no good.*

As one always seeking something better, however, Elizabeth listened with great interest to his tales of London. The English city sounded much better than Gothenburg. While he spoke, she ate all her dinner and gulped her vodka. Although she had frequently wanted to indulge, she hadn't had any of the drink since the time of her broken leg. Klaudio had bought a bottle and she allowed him to pour her a tall drink.

At first, the alcohol gave her a giddy vitality. The images that filled her head as he talked set her imagination ablaze. She was fascinated as he spoke about the English capital as the center of a vast global empire and a thriving mix of peoples from all over the world.

"The railway network," he said, "much greater than what we have in Sweden, links every corner of the British nation. Soon the steam-powered locomotives will also run through tunnels under the city of London. Everyone in the capital will ride a train wherever they want to go."

Klaudio's words stoked her desire for adventure, and a need to see more of the world. She smiled with delight, but suppressed her giggles for fear that Klaudio would look upon her as a silly child.

She craved more vodka, and as she kept drinking, the giddiness passed and was replaced by a sluggishness. Then, she was no longer hearing Klaudio's words. The tavern was hot and over-crowded. She became dizzy and nauseated. Elizabeth wondered how she could gracefully get away from Klaudio's monotonous rambling, which seemed to increase her discomfort by the minute.

Abruptly, she became certain she would vomit in the tavern if she didn't get out immediately and get some air.

"Is something wrong?" Klaudio asked, as she rose and headed for the door to the street, holding her hands over her mouth.

Patrons looked at her with surprise, concern, contempt.

Elizabeth made it to the street before her dinner came up. She crouched in the gutter to retch, the juices of her stomach, the food, and the drink burning her throat as it came up and kept coming in fits for several minutes.

Klaudio had not emerged from the tavern. Patrons going in or coming out gave her a wide berth. Elizabeth was disoriented. Her vision swam in a confusion of light and shadow. She'd never been so intoxicated. Her mother had never given her enough to do more than provide a soft euphoric feeling. Elizabeth didn't think she could stand without falling. Still crouched in the gutter, she kept her face down, her arms draped over her head in shame as the minutes passed and her intoxication deepened.

She heard footsteps, and then a hand gripped her left arm.

"They wouldn't let me leave until I'd paid," Klaudio said.

Elizabeth didn't care. She wanted to go home.

"Let me help you," he said.

She rose and was aware that she stumbled along beside him for a time as the night became darker and quieter.

Elizabeth awoke in a strange bed. Morning had come.

Her head had a throbbing ache and the dizziness remained. Her thoughts came through a fog. She felt a separation from herself.

Asleep, Klaudio lay naked beside her.

She was naked as well. The bedding beneath her was wet.

Elizabeth tried to remember what had happened, but there was nothing after the memory of him leading her away from the tavern.

She was wet between the legs. Something had dried in the hair of her crotch, leaving it matted and stiff. She touched the sticky wetness and saw red on her fingers.

Surely she was dreaming! Or had she been stabbed?

Of course you have, Liza said. *Klaudio did this to you.*

Elizabeth sat bolt upright, her senses suddenly too keen. The world around her pressed in with a reality that belied the suggestion of a dream. A small room with a single window surrounded her. The walls were a faded blue. The furnishings were spare, a table beside the bed, an old beaten-up wardrobe. Clothes were scattered on the floor—her clothes!

No, he could not have taken advantage of her as she slept.

No one would do that, Bess said. *He must be in love with you.*

Ridiculous, Liza said.

Elizabeth shook her head and the throbbing pain worsened.

I might become pregnant! If she became a mother so young, she'd be like so many women she'd known in life who were tied to one small community, increasingly dependent on others for her well-being and with little to look forward to but a dull existence of hard work.

Surely in a large city like Gothenburg, Liza said, *there are those who know how to take care of such things.*

Even in the small Hisingen farming community where she'd grown up, women whispered of methods of ending a pregnancy.

Elizabeth got up to fetch her clothes, and Klaudio stirred. She quickly slipped into her skirt and covered her breasts with her blouse and stockings.

"Why so shy?" Klaudio asked, sitting up in the bed.

Elizabeth backed up against the wall. She looked for a way out. The door was beyond his side of the bed.

"I—"

"You're frightened?"

"Yes." The word was barely a whisper as her shame roared in her head with the throbbing pain.

"No one will harm you."

"May I go home?"

"It's right next door."

Elizabeth realized she was at his home, next door to Fru Andersdotter's house.

"Your uncle—"

"Gone to sea."

Klaudio got up, donned his clothing while she watched. Increasing her unease, she noticed he was handsome without clothes too.

"I must go to the privy," he said. "If you are not here when I return, I hope to see you soon."

He exited the room and left the door open.

Elizabeth donned her clothing and walked in the late autumn chill across Ösp Lane to Hortense's house.

She discovered that morning had, in fact, long since passed. The house was cold since the fires had been allowed to go out. Hortense was sitting in the kitchen, bundled in the blankets from her bed. She had missed a meal because Elizabeth had not been there to prepare it for her. After hurrying to build a fire in the kitchen stove and in the fireplace in the parlor, Elizabeth sat the old woman down in the kitchen and fed her.

"I'm so sorry to have abandoned you," she said, but out of shame, she made no effort to explain further.

Hortense was silent for a moment, then said, "As long as you're happy, I'm not concerned. I know you needed to get away for a while." She smiled. "You are forgiven."

Elizabeth was grateful that Hortense didn't question her. The poor old woman had every right to be angry. Her gracious response made it all the more difficult for Elizabeth to forgive herself.

4

FOR HER TROUBLE

Elizabeth's horror at finding she'd lost her virginity to a relative stranger came less from moral outrage than from a sense that she'd been tricked out of a formative first experience. She wished she'd been awake and aware for the event. Although angry with Klaudio, and somewhat afraid of him, she'd been thinking about his naked body ever since.

As a child, Elizabeth had been baptized and confirmed in the Swedish Lutheran Church. She had studied the Small Catechism of Martin Luther, and taken the examination conducted by the Church, but her commitment to the religion was only as strong as that of her parents. They had shown no fervent belief through the years. Too busy perhaps making ends meet and raising their children, they had exhibited the bare minimum of devotion to the Church required to get along with others of the community.

One afternoon after a bath, she looked at her body in a mirror in her room, trying to determine if Klaudio had seen something in her he might want again. She was of average height, about five and a half feet tall, with curly light-brown hair and grey-green eyes. She was willowy, with a long neck, small breasts and a thin face. She still had the lips and nose of a young girl, but her eyes were quite attractive. Her right shin was bowed forward a bit and slightly lumpy where her broken tibia had not been set properly. At certain angles that could not be seen. Despite liking most of what she saw, she couldn't know if Klaudio had found her especially appealing.

He didn't come to see her. When coming and going from the house, Elizabeth hurried past his uncle's house to minimize the chance that she'd see him. As the cold, lonely months of November and December passed, though, her restlessness grew and in early January, she sought his company again.

Klaudio wanted to introduce her to a British merchant seaman friend, Mr. Robert Turner. The friend met them at The Siren's Promise. Mr. Turner was introduced to her as Robert.

Elizabeth had balked at the idea of returning to the tavern after her last performance there. Klaudio put her at ease, telling her they served so many people that surely they would not remember her. When they arrived at the tavern, she noticed that the establishment was much busier than the last time she visited. The air was filled with smoke that burned her eyes. As they looked for seating, Klaudio and Robert shouted their words to be heard over the raucous laughter and conversation that filled the place. Finally, they found a table in a cramped corner that was a bit less noisy.

Elizabeth had learned some English as a child from her aunt Tirtza, her father's older sister, who had served as a domestic servant in a British household when she was a young woman. Even so, she could not keep up with the conversation between Klaudio and his English friend. They made little effort to include her in their discussion.

Klaudio is still not interested in what you have to say, Liza said.

Yes, but you've caught the eye of the Englishman, Bess said. *Perhaps he will become fascinated with you, and carry you off to London where you can travel the city by rail.*

Robert was tall and dark-haired, with a thin face, sideburns and a turned up, boyish nose. He made an effort to speak with Elizabeth. Her stock phrases weren't much use. She understood many of the words he used, although they came too fast for her to keep up. Still, he smiled for her and glanced at her warmly from time to time.

Again, during dinner, Klaudio poured tall drinks from a bottle of vodka he ordered. Elizabeth wanted the exuberant feeling she'd got at first during the last meal at the tavern. She would avoid, however, going too far with her drinking and becoming ill. As she ate her meal, she sipped her drink even though she wanted to gulp it. When she was finished eating, although she wanted more vodka, she decided to quit for the night.

Klaudio poured more in her glass before she could think to stop him. She didn't drink from it. He seemed to notice, and made a toast in English she couldn't understand. When she didn't respond, he nudged her in a friendly manner, and said "Skål!"

"Cheers," Robert said, as Elizabeth reluctantly raised her glass. He downed the contents of his glass, a couple of ounces. When she took only a sip, both men balked and gestured for her to turn the glass up and drink it all.

Elizabeth wouldn't have them think she didn't know how to have a good time, so she took a larger drink. Still, vodka remained in her glass.

Klaudio wants you drunk, Liza said. *He will molest you again when you're helpless.*

Elizabeth didn't agree. The Englishman was with them. They were having a good time. The warmth of the drink was spreading through her in a comfortable manner and with it came an amorous feeling toward Klaudio. She thought of his naked form, the taper from his shoulder to hips, the muscular shapes of his legs and buttocks. Robert would eventually leave them—preferably sooner than later—and then, she'd be present and aware when the lovemaking began.

Klaudio poured a new round of vodka. When he got to Elizabeth's glass, she held her hand over it.

He smiled and set the bottle down.

"You're a pretty girl," Robert said, and he raised his glass. "Cheers."

"Thank you," Elizabeth said, but she made no move to take a drink.

The two men were insistent. She looked at the liquid in her glass, a larger amount than she'd thought.

Perhaps the effect will be less if you drink it quickly, Bess said.

Short of becoming ill, Elizabeth was so intoxicated she had difficulty focusing her senses and maintaining her physical coordination. She mistook one man for the other several times as they both helped to support and guide her through the cold, wintry air back to the house in Ösp Lane.

When finally she and her lover made it to bed and he penetrated her, the lovemaking was passionate and exciting, a long, slow exploration of the odors, flesh, and fluids of life itself. Finally, a moment came when a thrilling sensation gripped her, one that ebbed and flowed in waves of physical bliss before fading. Then, she lay spent until the dim world around her faded as well.

Elizabeth awoke much the way she had before, in the blue room with the table and the beaten-up wardrobe, but beside her was Robert. She leapt from the bed and scrambled after her clothing on the floor.

Klaudio had tricked her again!

Robert stirred and looked at her with a smile. "Good morning," he said, an English phrase she readily understood.

Elizabeth had nothing to say to him. She dressed, left the room, and sought Klaudio elsewhere in the house. She found him asleep upstairs in a bedroom, presumably his uncle's.

"What have you done?" she shouted.

He awoke startled, a confused look on his face. She waited for an answer as he shook his head and rubbed the sleep out of his eyes.

"You had a good time last night," he said. "Did you not?"

"No!"

"Robert had a good time. He likes you."

"I don't care what he likes!"

"I do," Klaudio said, raising his eyebrows. He slid open a drawer in the table beside the bed, took out a box, and opened the lid. The currency inside the box, mostly coins, was more money than Elizabeth had ever seen in one place.

She was confused—why would he count money in the middle of their conversation?

"Hold out your hands," he said. When she did, he dumped into them numerous silver and bronze coins. She could barely hold them all. Roughly counting the skilling and öre, she decided there was enough to make six riksdalers, an amount equal to half a week's wages at a menial job.

"This is what you earned for your trouble. I hope it's enough." He seemed genuinely concerned.

Elizabeth's anger turned to shame. She grimaced and folded her fingers over the handful of coins, already thinking about how she might spend them. Still holding her hands out before her,

Elizabeth backed away and left the room with her head bowed. Once out of Klaudio's presence, she dumped the money into a pocket in her top skirt. She fled down the stairs and left the house to return to Fru Andersdotter and belatedly prepare the old woman's early meal. She had a lie prepared about missing a ferry across the river and having to spend the night at the home of one of Klaudio's female cousins.

5

PROVIDENCE

Fru Andersdotter was dead, lying on the kitchen floor in her stained nightclothes. The old woman had been Elizabeth's friend, and she was gone.

The fires had gone out. In the January chill, the air in the house had become frigid, perhaps near to freezing. Hortense's face and chest were warm. Her hands were cold.

Elizabeth sat heavily on the floor beside the old woman and leaned back against the peeling wall. Coins spilled out of the pocket of her skirt and some rolled across the hardwood floor. She was in no hurry to put them back. Tears ran down her cheeks and into her blouse as she took the old woman's crooked hand in her own. She looked at Hortense, not knowing what to do.

I've failed her when she needed me most. No, I've killed her. I might as well have cut her throat.

She knew she would be blamed. To keep from suffering that blame, a remedy immediately came to mind: She would flee to

©2014

London, where she might be lost among the multitudes. But, then, she hadn't the funds to book passage.

If I'd listened to Liza, I might have left Klaudio last night and been here to help.

You'd have only stood in Fru Andersdotter's way, Bess said. *She got her wish. She's gone to heaven to be with her husband before the money ran out.*

The old woman was miserable and at death's door, Liza said, *and none of it was going to get any better. At least her suffering is at an end. Perhaps she left something for you in her will. Look through the house to see if you can find stray coins.*

Elizabeth didn't pay much attention to the voices. She was inconsolable. She hung her head and cried for Hortense and for herself.

Time passed and the house grew more chill. Elizabeth could not sit on the floor forever. She would have to go home.

No, there's nothing for me there. Caspar and Svein will eventually have the farm. It's already too small for one family. They won't want me there any more than Father does.

When she'd run out of tears, Elizabeth picked up her coins and stood. "I am a prostitute and a drunk," she said aloud as if confessing it to her dead friend, "and, soon, I'll be homeless. I must change before it's too late."

She felt the coins in her pocket, and considered giving them back to Klaudio.

No, she would need the money until she could find respectable work.

She had to tell someone of Fru Andersdotter's death.

Before you do, Liza said, *warm up the house so no one will know you were gone.*

Elizabeth took Liza's advice and started fires in the kitchen stove and in the fireplace in Hortense's bedroom. Then, going through the documents among the old woman's possessions, she found the name and address of the solicitor who managed the estate. Elizabeth donned her coat and a wool bonnet and set out through a cold, biting wind to visit the law office of Herr Roderick Rikhardsson. On the way, she stumbled over uneven cobblestones and fell, skinning her left knee. Mischievous boys, standing behind a short stone wall in a solemn neighborhood of dark brick houses, hurled rotten potatoes at her and laughed. She ran on to get away from them. The world had turned against her, Elizabeth decided, and she must work hard to redeem herself.

Even so, with Liza making suggestions, Elizabeth had a lie prepared in case she was questioned by the solicitor, one about waking up to find Hortense dead.

By mid-afternoon, at the end of a three and a half mile walk, she came to a small converted storefront. The place was much less substantial than she'd expected and she checked the address on the card she'd brought with her before going inside. Elizabeth supposed she was lucky he was there to receive her, since he had no clerk. His desk was piled so high with papers she didn't see him at first. He stood when he heard her footsteps. Herr Rikhardsson was an elderly gentleman with white hair, colorless eyes that looked sore, and a rumpled suit.

Following a brief introduction, Elizabeth found herself crying again as she told of Fru Andersdotter's death. "She had been coughing and complaining of chest pains," she lied, even though Herr Rikhardsson had shown no skepticism about her tale. Elizabeth was immediately ashamed of herself, and her sobbing became so uncontrollable that she was unable to go on with her story. She couldn't decide whether her tears were for the old woman or for herself.

Herr Rikhardsson helped her into a chair beside his desk. "I'm sorry to hear of it," he said. "She was a fine woman. When she was young, she went with our soldiers in their fight to enforce the Treaty of Kiel. She was a nurse, and Herr Rembert Bjorkman was a soldier she treated for a chest wound. She nursed him back to health, and then decided to keep him." Herr Rikhardsson pulled up a chair of his own, and sat, looking thoughtful. "That was long ago."

The old woman had never said much about her past. Elizabeth wished she'd shown more interest.

"You say you are Elizabeth Gustavsdotter. Do I understand, then, that you are the daughter of Beata Carlsdotter?"

"Yes."

"Hortense—" he hesitated. "Excuse me—I mean, Fru Andersdotter—she said you were coming."

"I've been here nearly four months."

"Your great-grandmother on your mother's side was her childhood friend."

He seemed to know much about the old woman. "If you knew her so well," Elizabeth asked with a sharp edge in her voice, "why didn't you help her?"

Herr Rikhardsson shook his head and looked down, an expression of hurt on his face.

Elizabeth was ashamed of herself—she was abusing him for the same reason she was angry with herself. "I'm sorry I spoke to you that way," she said.

"No, I understand. You're upset."

He was a kindly man, willing to expect the best in others. She was envious.

"Fru Andersdotter was too proud to take my help," he said. "She believed she had nothing to give me in return."

"Yes," Elizabeth said. "She was a modest woman."

"I imagine you don't know what you'll do now."

"I don't. I can't go home."

Herr Rikhardsson smiled tightly. "I have one more thing to give Fru Andersdotter. That is to say that I hope to give it to someone she cared about. I've been charged with finding a suitable young woman to take a position as a maid of all work for a gentleman, Herr Frederick-Lars Olovsson and his wife, Fru Joanna Ellstromsdotter. They have two small sons. Both parents are away from home much of the time. A monthman, he's gone for thirty days at a time. She's a personal maid in a fine household, and must stay over frequently. If you would take the position, you'd earn ten riksdalers, twelve skilling, and one öre per week. There is a nursemaid also with the household. You would room with her in the home."

Elizabeth was taken aback. She didn't expect providence to smile upon her in that moment.

Instead, I should suffer for what I did to the old woman.

You don't deserve the opportunity he offers, Liza said, *but he doesn't have to know that. You are always looking for* something better. *Well, here it is.*

Perhaps this is reward for some good you will do in the future, Bess said.

Elizabeth was eager to believe her innocent voice. *Perhaps if I learn to think of others first, I'll be able to forgive myself.* Indeed, her life was not over, and she would need to find some happiness in the world.

One large fear remained: If she won the house maid position of which Herr Rikhardsson spoke, and then discovered she was pregnant, she'd have to end the pregnancy before it showed or lose the position.

Hopefully, her luck would hold.

"Thank you, Herr Rikhardsson. I would like to be considered for the position."

6

EMPLOYMENT

The household of Frederick-Lars Olovsson was a modest, attractive two story wooden structure among houses and shops in the Majorna district, with three bedrooms upstairs, a nursery, parlor, small study, and kitchen downstairs. The lady of the house, Fru Ellstromsdotter, received Elizabeth in a business-like manner, and guided her through the home, explaining what would be expected of her. The woman was thin and pale, with dark hair pulled back tightly and secured at the back of her head with decorative pins. She had sharp facial features and her mouth opened crookedly when she spoke.

Elizabeth was shown the room she would share with the nursemaid. The chamber was not drafty, and the bed looked warm and comfortable.

"As a maid of all work," Fru Ellstromsdotter said, "you must cook all the meals, serve at mealtimes, change the bed linens, clean the house, haul water and slops, and share in the laundry duties."

Elizabeth was expecting the hard work, and felt up to it. She might have wished for an employer with a friendlier personality, however. Fru Ellstromsdotter had not offered a single smile or pleasant sentiment during the tour of the house.

"For the considerable sum offered," she said, "we expect constancy of service, and a minimum of requested absence. The children are everything to us. Pursuing two incomes as we do, we sacrifice our own presence in their young lives to secure their future and ensure that they have a happy, healthy, and safe home. We'll be fair with you, but you must accept that you're our inferior by virtue of the fact that we can afford to employ you. Your needs come after ours. As you must know, God, in his infinite wisdom, has fashioned such tests for all of us. My husband and I ceased to struggle against His will, and expect those within our household to do the same, for none of us are better than our God-given circumstances."

Elizabeth found Fru Ellstromsdotter words to be extraordinary, especially from one who's own circumstances were relatively modest. The wages offered for the position were certainly not sufficient to warrant such an attitude. Somehow, Elizabeth could not believe the woman meant what she said.

You should think twice about taking employment within this household, Liza said.

The woman merely expresses herself poorly, Bess said. *She will warm with time.*

Fru Ellstromsdotter looked Elizabeth in the eye as if awaiting a response. She merely nodded, and the woman tilted her head and widened her eyes as if to say she expected more of an answer.

"Yes, Fru Ellstromsdotter," Elizabeth said. "I understand."

"Then it's settled," the lady of the house said. "Welcome to our home."

She guided her new employee into the nursery to introduce the nursemaid and her children.

"These are my boys, Otto and Johan, one and two years of age

Her Olovsson is a good man, Bess said. *He's the sort who will look after you when you truly need help.*

"Thank you, Herr Olovsson."

"My wife knows nothing of how you came to us, and I will refrain from speaking to you in her presence, as I do with Fru Jensson. Please don't take offense from that. Fru Ellstromsdotter is a jealous woman. She had a hard life in her younger days and suffers the need to know just what belongs to her."

"I understand, Herr Olovsson," Elizabeth said. Concerning the demeanor of the woman of the house, however, she truly didn't understand—not yet.

As agreed, Elizabeth cooked, cleaned, kept the house, and helped with the laundry. Fru Ellstromsdotter did the shopping at market for their food on her way home from her work on Mondays. With a precious domestic servant position and plenty of children currently in her life, Elizabeth was more than relieved to find that she had not become pregnant. She was delighted with the children, yet glad she had no long-term responsibility toward them. During the long absences of both Herr Olovsson and Fru Ellstromsdotter, she worried that Otto and Johan would grow up not knowing their own parents. Despite the difficulties Elizabeth had with her own family members, she admitted to herself that she missed them.

The thought prompted her to begin the practice of writing to her mother once a week. She wrote of her experiences in Gothenburg, of her new position, and of the Olovsson family. She also told of the death of Fru Andersdotter, but Elizabeth conveyed nothing of her own activities during the incident. She received an answer perhaps once a month. Her mother's words, although not expressive, conjured images of home that surprisingly warmed Elizabeth's heart.

Living in Herr Olovsson's home was pleasant, if uneventful. Elizabeth gratefully remained warm and well-fed through the winter. By spring, the familiar restlessness was setting in. Remembering the troubles boredom had brought her in the past, she did her best to find happiness in her work. She stayed well away from alcoholic drinks.

Since her wages were small and she had little time to herself, Elizabeth spent few of her earnings on the occasions she went to market or browsed through shops in Gothenburg. As her funds accumulated, she decided that if she continued to save them, she would one day have enough to book passage to London. Whether she would merely visit the English capital or start a new life there, she was uncertain. She had no desire to stay in Gothenburg. The population of the city was increasing rapidly. The metropolis was dirty and over-crowded with the poor, most working low-wage industrial jobs. Crime abounded. The people were angry and in too much of a hurry.

Of one thing she was certain: working as a maid of all work would not be a long-term walk of life. Again, she wanted something better, and had hope that in England new opportunities would open for her.

The nursemaid, Leena Jensson, was twenty-four years old. Her family name, Jensson, unlike Elizabeth's patronym, Gustavsdotter, was a heritable one. The practice of giving heritable names had been gaining favor in the last few decades, especially among families dwelling in the city.

Leena's use of baby talk when speaking to children and adults alike continued, and Elizabeth began to think the woman spoke that way naturally. The baby talk reminded Elizabeth of Bess, but with none of the charm. She gritted her teeth every time she heard her name pronounced as Ewisabet.

"Please, call me Leena," the nursemaid said, and Elizabeth complied with difficulty, wanting instead to call her Weena.

Leena's personality matched her grating voice in many ways. Although Elizabeth tried to be friendly to her, she found spending time with the nursemaid tedious and irritating. Leena was frequently too childlike, her concerns simple and unambitious. Still, after Elizabeth's neglect of Hortense, she considered her relationship with the nursemaid a penance of sorts; a good opportunity to practice putting someone else's interests above her own. *If I can do that for Leena,* Elizabeth decided, *I can do it for anyone, and I'll be a better person for it.*

She saw Herr Olovsson rarely, and would speak to him in a conversational manner on four more occasions in the three years of her employment within the household, always at a time when Fru Ellstromsdotter was gone from the home in the afternoon. Each occasion, he asked for her to make him a cup of coffee. He sat in the kitchen and drank it while she worked, and asked her if she was happy and being treated well. She always assured him that she was.

"Yours is the best coffee I've ever had," he told her. "My morning coffee is never enough. When I'm away, and must drink the mud others make, I long for yours."

Her heart swelled with pride and she thanked him. She thought of her father who had always expressed appreciation for her coffee, if not for her alone. She imagined that Herr Olovsson would make a fine father when he could devote more time to his children.

"I can imagine a day when you're married to a man who loves your coffee as much as I do," Herr Olovsson said, "so much so that he drops whatever occupation he holds and opens a coffee shop. He will believe he's in charge, but he would have nothing without you, my dear."

Although Herr Olovsson laughed, Elizabeth liked his fanciful notion. She also liked being referred to as his "dear." If her father never noticed her worth, Herr Olovsson certainly did. Knowing she had his approval made her more tolerant of the man's cold, hard wife.

7

SMALL CONSPIRACY

One morning in May of 1861, while Elizabeth helped Leena fold linens, the nursemaid asked, "Will you keep a secret for me from our employer?"

Elizabeth didn't answer immediately. She was curious, though, since the woman had dropped her baby talk when asking for the favor.

"My mother is ill, suffering from grippe. I must go to her. I asked Fru Elstromsdotter for permission to do so, but she won't allow it. Since she'll be gone attending *her* lady overnight, I could leave for a time and she wouldn't know I was gone. If you'd keep the children during the evening, I would go see my mother and return around midnight."

Elizabeth appreciated that Leena was capable of talking to her like an adult.

Perhaps she dons the childish manner for effect, Liza suggested.

"What if she comes home early?" Elizabeth asked.

"She won't." Leena said flatly.

In the four months Elizabeth had worked for Fru Ellstromsdotter, the woman had returned in the evening only on one occasion when she'd said she'd be gone for the night. The reason given was that the noblewoman Fru Ellstromsdotter served had had to leave suddenly to be present for the birth of a granddaughter.

Elizabeth smiled and said she would keep the secret. She had few concerns beyond the possibility of being caught in a deception, and, since it was only short-term, she looked forward to being in charge of the children. When Leena returned home that night and their conspiracy remained a secret, Elizabeth was relieved.

In the months that followed, the nursemaid asked for the same favor several times. As Elizabeth became skeptical of the woman's consistent excuse, Leena explained. "My mother has had problems with her health ever since I was born. I do my best for her."

"I worry—"

"Yes," Leena interjected, "but the hazard is truly mine."

"I'm not certain what I should say if Fru Elstromsdotter comes home while you're gone."

"You should say whatever seems reasonable."

She's certainly confident, Liza said.

Because Elizabeth was sympathetic and willing to hold her secret, Leena took the habit of leaving one night a week to visit her mother.

Life within the Olovsson household was so boring that Elizabeth found herself vicariously enjoying the nursemaid's risk.

Fru Ellstromsdotter came home unexpectedly on an evening in

the autumn of 1861, and asked about the nursemaid's absence.

Liza had a simple lie prepared for Elizabeth. "Someone called at the house to say that her mother had taken ill. I told her I would take care of your sweet boys until she returned."

Fru Ellstromsdotter was satisfied, but obviously unhappy with the news. Although something about her manner suggested she felt thwarted in some way, she didn't give voice to it.

When Leena returned, she acted not the least surprised to see the lady of the house.

Fru Ellstromsdotter asked after the nursemaid's mother.

"She was feeling a little better when I left her," Leena said. "I'm sorry I left so suddenly. I believe I left the children in good hands." She nodded toward Elizabeth.

"I expect this is something that won't happen again."

"Yes, Fru Ellstromsdotter," Leena said, "you can expect that."

The nursemaid lowered her eyes and head in a submissive stance. While Leena wasn't speaking to the lady of the house in baby-talk, her words were simple and her tone that of a guileless young girl.

She's knows just what to say and how to behave to avoid punishment, Liza said.

As Elizabeth cleaned the nursery the next day, she spoke to Leena. "I don't feel good about lying to Fru Ellstromsdotter."

"I understand," Leena said. She rocked the children in their cribs with the hope that they might nap through the afternoon. "Perhaps I can make it worth your while by giving you my wages for the hours you stand in for me."

Elizabeth found the deal attractive and agreed. Leena had ceased to use baby-talk when in conversation with Elizabeth. Liza had been right when she suggested that the nursemaid donned the innocent face, complete with baby-talk, for effect. Elizabeth had broken through to the genuine Leena, and they were becoming friends.

What had been a once per week occurrence became more frequent, however. In the summer of 1862, Leena was caught missing again. Elizabeth told Fru Ellstromsdotter the same story she had the last time, then added a detail she regretted. "The doctor came for her this time."

The lady of the house had a look of skepticism. Elizabeth shrugged. Fru Ellstromsdotter shook her head slowly and turned away.

Belatedly, Elizabeth realized that a doctor would not leave a gravely ill patient to run such an errand.

When Leena returned, the lady of the house demanded to know why she'd left.

"I'm very sorry, Fru Ellstromsdotter," Leena said. "My mother was ill again. She suffers pleurisy after a bout with pneumonia." Gesturing toward Elizabeth, she said, "Again, I left your precious ones in capable hands."

Fru Ellstromsdotter had a stiffness about her, as if a rebuke stood on the tip of her tongue, but apparently she couldn't find a reasonable argument against the compassionate grounds for Leena's absence.

"Did the doctor come for you?" she asked Leena, her words short and sharp.

The nursemaid glanced at Elizabeth too briefly to communicate anything. "No, Fru Ellstromsdotter, his assistant."

The lady of the house looked at Elizabeth suspiciously. Following an awkward silence, she said to Leena, "In the future, you must send word to me before leaving the house."

"Yes, Fru Ellstromsdotter," the nursemaid said.

The lady of the house turned to Elizabeth. "At the very least, *you* should have sent word that Fru Jensson had been called away."

"Yes, Fru Ellstromsdotter," Elizabeth said. She lowered her

eyes and then her head the way she'd seen Leena do.

"Now, off to bed with the both of you," the lady of the house demanded.

Elizabeth was unhappy that Fru Ellstromsdotter had become upset with her for Leena's deception. Since the nursemaid was paid little more than Elizabeth, the added income from the deal they'd struck didn't amount to much.

While taking a break from washing pots and pans in the kitchen to allow more water to heat on the stove, she sought Leena in the nursery. Elizabeth found her sitting on the floor with the children, playing with soft dolls she'd made from yarn and telling a story about them. Although the toddlers couldn't understand the tale, they gave her all their attention. Elizabeth smiled to think that Leena genuinely cared for the children.

When a pause occurred in Leena's story, Elizabeth said, "I'm sorry, but the extra income is not worth the risk. If Fru Ellstromsdotter finds out I'm lying to her, I'll lose my position. She will understand if you explain about your mother's continuing illness."

"No," the nursemaid said, looking up, "she won't. I once tried to take a day to see my sister married, and she would have none of it. She is a woman of humble origins who never expected to have servants. She likes it too much, and prefers to think she owns us."

Because Elizabeth had not had such experiences with Fru Ellstromsdotter, she couldn't argue with Leena. The lady of the house was a hard woman.

Leena's lips pinched together as though she were considering something, then she said, "I'll give you two riksdaler each time I go out."

That was a day's wages. Elizabeth knew her eyes had become wide and her mouth had dropped open.

She is up to something besides visiting her mother, Liza said. *Still, that's a good deal. Don't question her, just accept it.*

We'll become rich enough within a year to book passage to England, Bess said.

Elizabeth merely nodded her head for Leena.

Elizabeth began watching out for Leena's return on the nights the nursemaid was out of the house. Once the children were safe in bed, she'd sit in the shadows of her upstairs bedroom where the view from windows allowed her to see up and down the lane in front of the house. She was becoming weary of the practice after a couple of months of seeing the nursemaid return alone. Finally, in the autumn of 1862, she saw a carriage arrive in the lane perhaps one hundred yards away from the house to the west. At first she thought the vehicle was a coach for hire. Then, as Leena and a man stepped down from it, Elizabeth determined that the man had been driving. They stood among the shadows of a shopfront, kissing for some time, then Leena left him and made her way inside.

Her lover must mean the world to her, Bess said. *If the carriage belongs to him, he is certainly a prosperous fellow.*

Thinking of all she'd earned from Leena since they'd struck their new deal, Elizabeth was fascinated by the idea that a man could be worth so much to a woman. The possibility existed that the money she received to keep Leena's secret came from him. Elizabeth wanted to get a good look at the fellow. She continued her vigil through the winter and into the year of 1863. As the months passed, she did see Leena with the man, sometimes arriving on foot, sometimes by carriage. Elizabeth couldn't quite make out his features. One night in late summer, he looked a bit shorter than usual.

She has a new lover, Bess said, *one who loves her even more than the last.*

That didn't seem right.

Keep watching, Liza said, her suspicion obvious, but uncomfortable.

On a night in December of 1863, an older man seemed to stand in the shadows kissing Leena, and Elizabeth came to a conclusion she didn't want to accept, yet was hard avoid.

She stopped looking out for the woman's return, kept her suspicion to herself, and continued to take the nursemaid's money.

In February 1864, Fru Ellstromsdotter again came home unexpectedly in the evening.

Elizabeth was in a panic because she didn't want to lose the currently substantial income from Leena. She thought better of giving the same excuse as before, and told Fru Ellstromsdotter that Leena's mother had been taken to the hospital. Inspired by her own fall, Elizabeth said, "I believe she fell from a height and broke her leg."

The lady of the house looked at her in disbelief. "Fru Jensson's mother is of advanced age," she said. "She would not be scaling any heights." She was quiet for a moment, then donned her cloak and left the house in a rush.

Elizabeth was relieved until she realized that the hospital was not far away. Her dread built in intensity until the lady of the house returned. Leena entered the house with Fru Ellstromsdotter. The nursemaid's head was downcast.

Elizabeth tried to catch Leena's eye, but couldn't.

"For your lies, I am terminating your employment, Fru

Gustavsdotter," Fru Ellstromsdotter said, glaring at Elizabeth. "And you'll receive no references from me." She seemed to compose herself before continuing. "Fru Jensson has persuaded me to allow you to stay the night. Tomorrow she will take you to her mother's home where you may stay briefly until you find other lodgings."

Elizabeth opened her mouth to speak and Fru Ellstromsdotter slapped her across the face. "I'll hear no more from you. If you try to speak again within my home, I'll put you out immediately. Now, go to bed."

Elizabeth followed the nursemaid to their room. If Herr Olovsson had been home, she might have considered taking the problem to him and pleading for her job. He had left within the week and wouldn't return for almost a month.

Once the door to their room was closed, Leena spoke to her in a whisper. "Why did you tell her my mother broke her leg?"

Elizabeth was mortified with embarrassment. She sat on her bed and Leena sat next to her.

"I thought she needed to believe your mother was in great danger to justify your absence. I didn't think she'd find out I was lying."

"I'm so sorry," Leena said. "I know you were trying to help."

"I'm sorry I failed you. What will *you* do?"

"I'll be fine," the nursemaid said. "I still have my position."

Elizabeth opened her mouth to say something, but was speechless.

You covered for the woman, and now you'll suffer for it, Liza said. *She continues to deceive you. That's what comes from placing other's interests above your own.*

At least you earned something for your trouble, Bess offered.

"She went to the hospital," Leena said, "then came to my mother's home. She could see that my mother is ill."

Elizabeth turned and looked her in the eye. "You're a prostitute!" she said, her expression showing anger while her words were whispered.

Leena hung her head. "Yes," she said. "I could not afford to take care of my mother otherwise. I was with my mother, not a man tonight. Lucky for me, since Fru Ellstromsdotter came to our door."

Her mother was indeed ill—Elizabeth finally understood. She took Leena's hand, and the nursemaid turned and hugged her.

"You can stay with my mother for a few days. Then, if you'd like, I can introduce you to someone who can find work for you, the work I do some nights."

"That's illegal!"

"Yes, yet it's tolerated in the city. The police help regulate it to prevent the spread of disease. Good positions are difficult to find, but a woman can easily earn her keep as a prostitute."

Elizabeth turned away without a response. She put on her nightclothes, crawled in her bed, and tried unsuccessfully to sleep.

As she tossed and turned, she thought about the opinions, insights, and advice given by Bess and Liza Black Tongue.

Do they cause more problems than they help solve, she wondered.

The two internal voices were as often wrong as they were right. Hearing from them was much like listening to any friend, family member, or even a stranger; everything they had to say was colored by formative experiences.

Bess's messages were ones of hope, the perspective she offered often allowing Elizabeth to see beauty and the hopeful possibilities ahead in life. Liza's messages were ones of fear, her mistrustful perspective helping to warn Elizabeth of real dangers on occasion.

Reality often lay hidden between their opposing points of view. Bess had told Elizabeth the first man she'd seen with Leena was the nursemaid's lover. If Elizabeth hadn't accepted that warm idea, her suspicions about the woman's motives might have been raised. Liza had warned her not to question Leena's motives for offering the most recent financial deal for fear that Elizabeth's conscience might get in the way.

Of course she could no more shut off the voices that arose unbidden in her mind than she could shut off the sun. She considered attempting to ignore them, but that didn't seem possible either, since frequently they blended together and were indistinguishable as anything save Elizabeth herself.

Elizabeth decided she must depend on both Bess's and Liza's perspectives. Each voice contributed a different form of defense through flawed counsel.

Concerning her question about whether Bess and Liza solved more problems than they caused, no clear answer presented itself. Elizabeth was exhausted at dawn, when the nursemaid roused her from bed.

She could see no other course but to follow Leena to her mother's home, and to take her voices with her.

8

PROSTITUTION

Lena sent Elizabeth to a cafe in the Haga district to meet the man who could help her find work. The nursemaid referred to him as Klaus.

Although the door to the establishment was open, and the time was well past noon, the place seemed unusually quiet for a cafe. As she stepped inside, the low murmur of conversations within ceased. Once her eyes adjusted to the dim interior, she saw that the place was filthy. A young girl was making a halfhearted effort to sweep dirt and ash from the floor. The tables were hopelessly spattered and stained. A broken chair crouched in the walkway. Eight women—a sullen lot—occupied three tables near the entrance. They appeared to be permanent fixtures rather than patrons. Elizabeth got the impression they waited for something, as if their day had not yet begun. Several of the women gave her assessing glances full of resentment before returning to desultory conversations.

Elizabeth made her way around the broken chair, and found a man seated at a table in a corner of the cafe. His head was down as he went over figures in a small book. She knew the man must be Klaus, but when he saw her and looked up, he had the blonde hair, strong nose, and square jaw of Klaudio. Herr Lydersson *was* Klaudio. She was startled by the realization, yet he appeared to have been expecting her. He gestured for her to join him.

Without taking a seat and offering no greeting, she asked Klaudio, "Did you believe you would see me again?"

"You should not speak to me that way," he said coldly. "To answer your question, yes." He shrugged. "I could see it in your eyes when last we met."

Elizabeth knew he thought she was easy to manipulate, and that he had no compunction about doing so. She wanted to turn and walk out immediately. She was not his whore!

Or was she? Why shouldn't he think that? She'd taken money from him for sex once before.

Elizabeth had resisted Leena's suggestion that prostitution was gainful employment. After a short stay with the nursemaid's mother, she'd found a room in a tenement and then tried to find work. Within a short time, she had spent all the money she'd saved and still had no employment. At present, Elizabeth was hungry, and didn't know how she'd pay for lodging.

She sat heavily at the table across from Klaudio.

"I can get you a room and clients," he said.

She was quiet for a long time, and he waited patiently. The employment he offered was certainly not something better than what she'd had. Unable to put a rosy glow on Elizabeth's future, even Bess was silent. Finally, Elizabeth lowered her head into her hands on the coffee-stained tabletop and said, "Tell me everything I'll need to know."

The room was damp and drafty, located in a crooked wooden house on Pilgatan Street, Eastern Haga. The chamber was furnished with a small metal stove against one wall, a rickety table, a small cabinet, a wash tub, chamber pot, ewer, basin, and a bed with a sagging straw mattress infested with mice. To protect food from the rodent pests, she stored what little she kept in the room in the cabinet with her clothing. While she slept, mice frequently congregated on or around the cabinet, trying to get to the food. As she stirred upon awakening, she'd hear them scurrying away.

Klaudio insisted that Elizabeth wash her hair with paraffin once a week to remove lice. She was also required to leave a residue of the fuel in her hair to discourage the parasites. To make the treatment more tolerable for both herself and clients, she perfumed her hair.

"Fru Jensson did not suffer such indignities to work for you," Elizabeth said to Klaudio.

"You know little of her," he said. "She has a way about her that draws a certain clientele. With time, you might develop such a gift, but at present, you're learning the ropes and can't be trusted on the street."

The only characteristics Lena had that stood out in Elizabeth's memory were her baby-talk and childlike ways. *If those are what Klaudio refers to, that doesn't seem like something a man would want.*

For the next year, nearly all her days and nights were taken from Elizabeth by strange men, often fouled by poor hygiene, disease, parasites, mental instability or simply alcohol. They came to her room from the waterfront, where Klaudio found clients among the seamen of various nationalities coming ashore while their ships were in port. Her respite came when a client wanted only to talk. She was grateful for the talkative ones, and was sure to show she was listening, even when their words meant nothing to her, even when they spoke a language she could not understand and they knew it. With or without sex, they paid Klaudio the same. Those who came only to talk were the least likely to beat her.

Elizabeth kept a supply of both vulcanized rubber and sheep's gut sheaths for men to wear while having sexual intercourse. Many would not wear them, and she learned quickly not to demand it. Some withdrew prior to climax. When a man ejaculated inside her, however, she douched as soon as possible with a solution provided by Klaudio that left her nauseated.

The pay she received per client was a small fraction of what she'd been given for sex with Robert Turner.

Early on, Klaudio had explained, "On that occasion I was presenting the Englishman with an innocent. You weren't a virgin—I'd taken that—but your bearing was certainly that of an innocent, and that was what he paid for. You no longer bear yourself in that manner. Life has taken that from you, and I cannot sell you for more than I've indicated. And, of course, my share, and the cost of your room, board, and fuel for your stove comes out of what is paid."

Elizabeth found Klaudio's confidence infuriating, yet compelling. Although she hated him, she'd never been more attracted to the man. She wanted to make love to him and then drown him in the Göta river. When Klaudio was good to Elizabeth, buying her new clothing, a meal at a good tavern or merely complimenting her appearance, her heart swelled with warmth for him, and Liza would warn her that his actions were all part of his continued manipulation. When he was the cruel ponce, withholding her pay, striking her in places least likely to cause bruising, or simply berating her for not pleasing a client, her rage boiled up—a reaction she could not show the man—and Bess would calm her with hopes of getting away and going to England to live.

Bess had once quietly hinted that Klaudio might change, take a tender interest in her, and they'd find true love. The suggestion sent Elizabeth into a worse rage, one turned upon herself, with recriminations of hopeless naiveté, of stupidity, and of worthlessness. The bout of anger, like so many others she had while under Klaudio's thumb, turned to a deep melancholy as she saw no way out of her situation.

I would not be here if I had treated Fru Andersdotter better.

As advised, Elizabeth was truthful with the police about her occupation and was registered with them as a prostitute in March of 1865. They kept a watch on her, periodically coming to her room to inspect it and question her.

The older woman living in the room next door was named Ada. She also worked for Klaudio. Ada always looked unhappy. She was dirty and unkempt. The first time they'd spoken to one another, Elizabeth had lied to her. "I'm working for Klaudio only until my family is settled in London, England," she'd said. "Then they'll send for me to join them."

She'd known even as she said it that the lie wasn't believable. The older woman had covered a smile with her hand, and turned away.

She will think you are too proud, Liza said.

After that, Ada shunned her. That suited Elizabeth perfectly well, since the woman represented a disturbing mirror into which she feared to gaze.

Even so, Elizabeth needed someone with experience to consult. As the months passed, she felt ill with increasing frequency, and suffered a chronic soreness within her abused and swollen vagina. She knocked on Ada's door, and asked her to suggest a remedy. Ada invited her into the room. The place reeked of stale sex, unwashed linens, and dirty clothes.

Ada took a tin of ointment out of a chest beside her bed, and offered it reluctantly. "Use this for the pain."

The salve helped a little.

Having missed her monthly flow twice, Elizabeth sought Ada's advice again.

"There's nothing wrong with you, *foolish girl*," Ada said, reminding Elizabeth of her mother. "You're pregnant. Better do something quick before Klaus finds out."

Elizabeth had suspected as much. Feeling something of Bess, she had a thrill at the thought that a life grew inside her. Then, something of Liza made her see the impossibility of bringing an infant into her world.

Ada wrote out a name and address on a piece of paper and handed it to her. "This is where you should go."

Elizabeth was too frightened to follow the woman's advice, afraid for the child and for herself. She saved the slip of paper, but allowed time to pass. Despite knowing she would not be welcome on the farm, especially in the condition in which she found herself, she considered running away from Klaudio and returning to her family.

When she'd first taken the room, Elizabeth had written to her mother with her new address, and their correspondence continued. Eight months after taking up prostitution, she was still pretending for her mother that she worked as a domestic servant in the Olovsson household. She didn't write about her pregnancy.

Apparently, her mother was withholding the truth as well. The woman had been suffering for some time. Elizabeth found out about it from her father, as she sat on the lumpy mattress in her room one afternoon in April, reading the first letter she had ever received from him.

Dear Daughter Elizabeth,

I'm sad to write to tell you that your dear mother has passed away. She had been having chest pains for several months but was unwilling to see the doctor. Her thoughts were with you and your sister with the hope that you are doing well. I too hope you are prospering in the city.

Caspar and Svein have ambitions beyond Hisingen.

Now that my dear Beata is gone, I will finish the year and then try to sell the farm.

Please send me news.

Regards from my heart,
Herr Gustav Ericsson

Soon there would be no place and no family to run to.

Caspar and Svein are smart to dream of something greater, Liza said.

Elizabeth had no desire to write to her father. She was furious with her mother. How dare she withhold her illness. *I might have seen you one last time!* She pounded the mattress in frustration, upsetting the most recent litter of mice within.

Listening to their tiny cries, Elizabeth fell forward and wept. She knew that feeling sorry for herself wouldn't help anything, but she couldn't resist the idea that she meant little to her family and nothing at all to anyone else in the world.

You hold within, one who will love you dearly someday, Bess said.

After a time, Elizabeth rolled over and considered the slight swell of her belly. No, having had a hard time merely providing for herself, she didn't want to become a mother. Still, she had hidden her pregnancy from Klaudio for fear that he would harm the child and herself trying to force a miscarriage.

A knocking came from her door, the insistent rhythm the police used when they wanted to inspect her room. Elizabeth got up and answered the door. Police Constable Lindquist stood in the threshold. He pushed his way inside as Elizabeth backed away to make room.

She liked him. He was young, somewhat handsome, and he'd treated her with some small respect. Both Elizabeth's inner voices had thought he might be a valuable ally in helping her get away from Klaudio, Liza suggesting she use the lure of sex and Bess proposing that Elizabeth should make him fall in love with her.

The Police Constable looked her up and down. He seemed different somehow, and then she realized that the difference was how he looked at her.

"Herr Lydersson has sent me for my share," he said awkwardly.

"Money?" Elizabeth asked.

"No," he said, taking a deep breath. He had a timid look as he reached for her.

Now's your chance, Liza said.

Elizabeth allowed him to guide her gently back onto the bed. He slowly undressed her. Although she had long since lost her discomfort when naked around men, she was embarrassed as he looked at her. He had such a little-boy-gawking expression.

Elizabeth backed up onto the mattress as he undressed, never taking his eyes off her.

Don't be afraid, Bess said. *He looks at you with love in his eye.*

Finally, he climbed onto the bed with a massive erection. "Please, spread your legs," he said.

As she complied, he hungrily looked toward her crotch.

A sour expression twisted his features and he withdrew, stood, and reached for his clothing. "Dress yourself, Fru Gustavsdotter. I must take you to Kurhuset."

Elizabeth's heart beat rapidly in her chest. "What have I done?" she asked, fear of the unknown rising.

He's arresting you, Liza said.

"Nothing," he said, a sorrow in his voice. "You've done nothing, but you have a chancre."

9

KURHUSET

On her way out with Police Constable Lindquist, Elizabeth had seen Ada going to her room, and told her she was being taken to Kurhuset. Ada gave her a sad smile that did nothing to ease Elizabeth's fears.

All the sick prostitutes went for treatment at Kurhuset. The facility was in Eastern Haga, a half mile away from Elizabeth's room. As she walked with the constable, she suffered the worst her imagination could offer. She'd seen a woman afflicted with syphilis who had lost her nose and lips, and she knew of other sufferers whose legs and arms were so ravaged by ulcers the limbs had to be amputated.

Halfway to Kurhuset, she felt unusually painful cramping. She thought perhaps her monthly flow had resumed, and had a small hope that she was not pregnant after all. By the time they arrived at Kurhuset, Elizabeth's skirts were stained with blood. Although he clearly noticed the stains, Constable Lindquist had the courtesy to say nothing. She swallowed her pride, calmed her fears, and entered the building.

The large structure was cold inside. The echoes of sounds off the hard walls and high ceilings were startling. The efficient and business-like behavior of the staff was intimidating.

Steel yourself to endure their scorn, Liza said.

Contrary to what her cynical voice suggested, Elizabeth was treated respectfully. She was asked numerous questions and notations were made of her answers. Eventually, she was led by a red-headed female dressed in starched blue cotton to a small, clean room furnished with a table and cabinets along the walls.

"Fru Gustavsdotter," the assistant said, glancing at the piece of paper in her hand, "I am Fru Finberg, assistant physician. Please take off your clothes, put them in the basket in the corner, and wear this." She handed Elizabeth a light cotton robe. "Then lie back on the table with your knees bent."

Elizabeth climbed onto the hard, wooden surface and tried to become comfortable, a difficult task as boney as she had become in recent months.

Fru Finberg stood at the end of the table and spread Elizabeth's legs. "You have an unusual quantity of blood flow," she said with a frown. "Are you experiencing the beginning of your menstrual cycle?"

"Yes, it always begins that way," Elizabeth lied, feeling embarrassed. Again, she was relieved to think she wasn't pregnant.

Fru Finberg cleaned the blood away. "The chancre is small and soft. The evidence is insufficient to make a determination of syphilis, but treatment should have a good effect."

A small hope peeked out from behind Elizabeth's large fear. "I'm certain it's an insect bite," she lied. "There's nothing else it could be."

Fru Finberg looked for a moment as if she might contest the statement, then simply shook her head.

She will be able to cure your ills, Bess advised.

If the cure doesn't make you worse, Liza warned.

The assistant physician applied an ointment to the chancre and the surrounding area, and gave Elizabeth a dose of a clear liquid to drink.

"You'll be given a quantity of the ointment and quinine to take with you when you return home," Fru Finberg said. "You'll also be given instructions on how to use the medicine and when you must return for another examination. You are required to present a report to the police after each examination. Your clothes will be burned, and we will give you fresh clothing to wear home. Your clothes and bedding at home should be thoroughly washed or burned. Please, climb down and I'll give you clothing."

As Elizabeth slid off the edge of the table, she felt something slippery issue from between her legs. The texture was different from the ointment. She stood and turned to see a slimy substance, streaked with brown and red, clinging to the edge of the table. Abruptly, an amber liquid with an odd smell poured from her onto the floor.

"Back onto the table, please," the startled assistant physician said. She helped Elizabeth back up and began another examination.

I'm coming apart! Elizabeth took sharp, short breaths, a panic welling up, along with a severe abdominal pain.

"You are pregnant, Fru Gustavsdotter."

"No, I couldn't be," Elizabeth said with no conviction.

"That's often not for us to decide," Fru Finberg said. "Are you experiencing pain?"

"Yes, but it's subsiding." Elizabeth lied to both the assistant physician and to herself. "I ate some bad fish. I'm sure that's all it is."

"I'll return in a moment," Fru Finberg said, and she left the room in a hurry.

Pain kept Elizabeth on the table, and the moment stretched to the unseen horizon of her life. What would she do with another mouth to feed? How could she do all that she must to protect and love a child when she could hardly take care of herself? As difficult as that seemed, she wondered if the child might be her way out of her situation with Klaudio. He would not want her to keep the child, but she didn't think he'd want the trouble that would come from trying to separate her from it. She could always seek alms from the Church.

Fru Finberg returned ten minutes later with a pale, dark-haired woman.

"This is Fru Dahlgren," she said. "She's a midwife."

"Good evening, Fru Gustavsdotter," the woman said as she went to work.

Elizabeth didn't respond because the idea of a greeting under such circumstances seemed foolish.

Fru Dahlgren positioned herself between Elizabeth's legs at the end of the table and began an uncomfortable examination. The midwife moved to the side, placed a pinard horn on Elizabeth's abdomen and listened, then changed the position of the device and listened again. Fru Dahlgren shook her head. "Labor has come early. You're four months pregnant?"

"I've missed my monthly flow for five at least," Elizabeth said.

"Labor has begun. I can't detect a heartbeat."

Elizabeth had a sinking feeling in her gut.

"You must prepare yourself for a stillbirth," the midwife said. "I'll be here to help you deliver."

She had lost her child before either of them had been given a chance. Was that nature's way of protecting the innocent from a life of suffering or had the infant, in fact, rejected its own mother as unfit? No, Elizabeth would have cleaned herself up, got honest work and been a loving mother.

Fru Finberg held out a hand and Elizabeth took it and hung on until her labor was over.

When she saw the dead child, she felt a depth of loss she hadn't expected. The assistant physician asked if she wanted the child's name to be recorded in the Kurhuset records.

Elizabeth said without hesitation, "Beata Gustavsson."

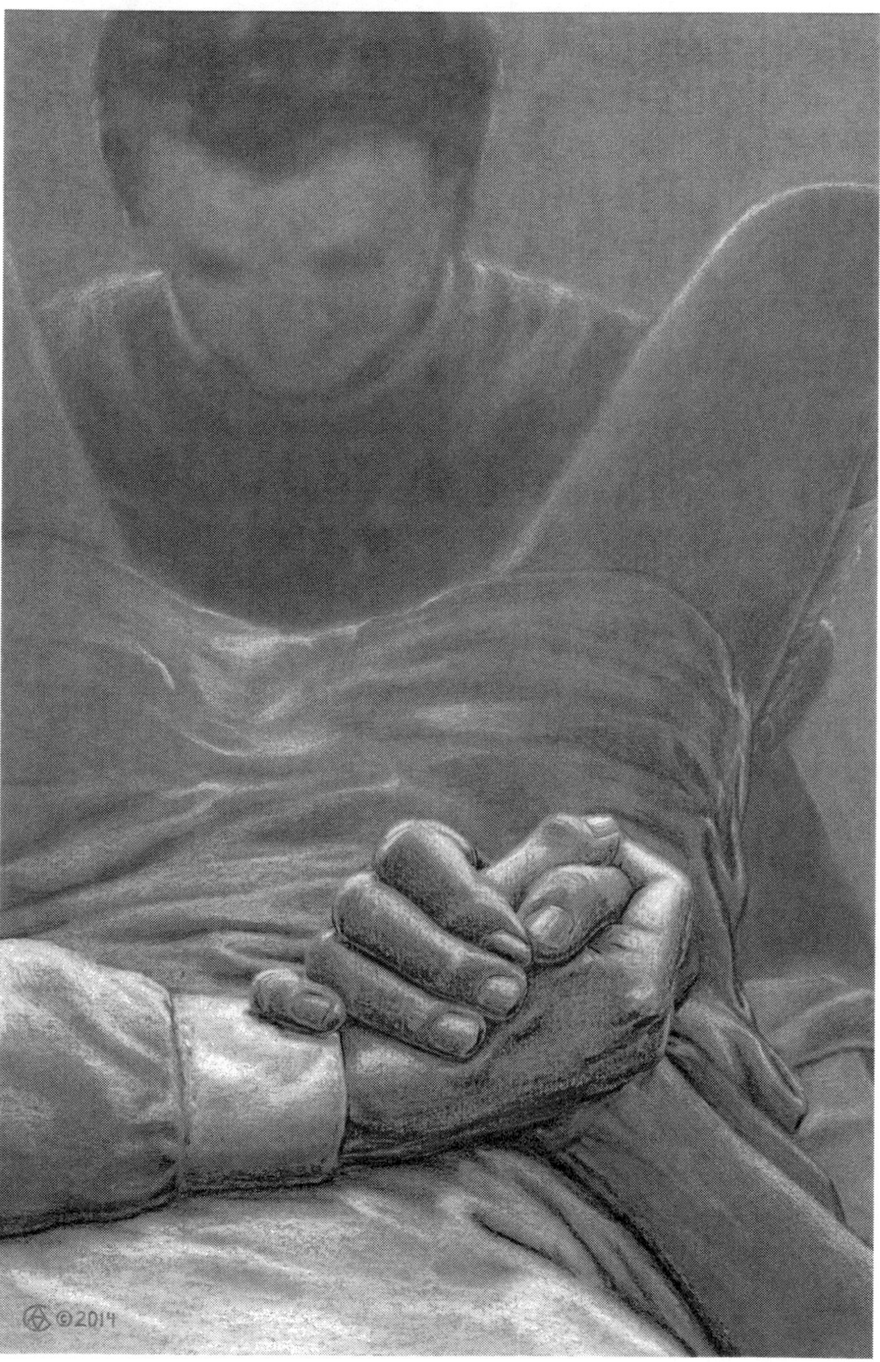
©2014

10

DRASTIC MEASURES

Elizabeth did not believe the expressions of sympathy Klaudio gave her upon hearing of her visit to Kurhuset and the loss of her infant. He was visiting her in her room. He'd brought her blood sausage and bread.

"You must become well before I can send more clients to you," he said. He looked around her miserable chamber. "I'll send Ada to help you clean. Within a few days you'll be better."

In the next week, she had two appointments for examinations. Elizabeth was ambivalent about how fast she hoped to be cured; she wanted the disease gone as quickly as possible, but every day she suffered meant at least six less clients she'd have to satisfy.

When Klaudio had gone, Ada appeared at her door. She'd cleaned herself up. "He will let me take two days off if you'll allow me to help you. Please?"

"Of course," Elizabeth said, allowing her to enter.

Ada helped Elizabeth haul water and wash her clothes and

bedding. Unexpectedly, they got along well. Ada was also from a farming family in Torslanda. Her family had fallen on hard times and she had come to the city for work. The future she portended for Elizabeth was frightening, for although merely seven years older, Ada looked to be middle-aged. Her hair was thinning, her skin and hooded eyes jaundiced, and her outlook on life was bleak.

Ada had brought with her a poison cereal to kill the mice. "Poor little creatures," she said as she sprinkled the lethal grains around the cabinet in Elizabeth's room. "They're just hungry."

"Like us," Elizabeth said sadly.

"Well, no," Ada said, looking up with an expression of exaggerated sobriety. "They'll eat anything. This is raw corn. *We* have sophisticated taste. To poison me, one would have to tempt me with warm buttered dumplings and blueberries." Ada gave a large gap-toothed smile. "Now that I've lost most of my teeth, I can eat all the sweets I want."

Elizabeth smiled, thinking of her favorite Christmas dinner. "For me, ham and lingonberry jam!"

The two women laughed together. The good humor from Ada was unexpected, and gave Elizabeth a glimpse of what the woman might have been like under happier circumstances.

Elizabeth decided that she liked Ada.

If you let her, she will become a good friend, Bess said.

In the following week Elizabeth kept her appointments at Kurhuset, after which she carried her examination reports to the police station. Since her condition didn't improve, more appointments were required. Klaudio allowed her more time to recover.

Once the adult rodents were killed by Ada's poison, the

squeals of baby mice inside Elizabeth's mattress continued for a while. A short time later their cries ceased. Within a week her bed began to smell of rotting flesh.

At first she believed she was responsible for the odor as her condition worsened, the chancre on her vulva became hard, red, granular, and gave forth a pungent smell. Miserable with sore muscles and aching joints, she remained in bed most of the time.

When possible, Ada helped her to and from Kurhuset and the police station.

At best, the treatment for her chancre helped prevent the disease from spreading. By mid-August, the disease had taken hold. Following an examination on August 13, she was put into a ward with other women suffering from syphilis.

Curtains kept Elizabeth from seeing the worst of the suffering. The sounds and smells, however, were demoralizing. The moans of those in agony kept her awake at night. She drifted through her days in an uncomfortable half-stupor from lack of sleep. She found none of the other women in any condition to socialize. If she started a conversation, her partner invariably used the opportunity to express misery or anger. She decided that most of the patients had gone mad.

Elizabeth's treatments continued, but with a new ointment, one made from cacao butter and mercury, applied four times a day, as well as daily oral doses of quinine. When no improvement was seen after a week, the quinine was replaced with oral doses of mercury sublimate.

The doctors are trying to kill you, Liza said.

The treatment is a drastic measure for a severe illness, Bess said. *If you're patient, they'll make you well again.*

Elizabeth's limbs swelled and her skin had a painful itch. Her toes and fingertips became bright pink and sore to the touch. On occasion, her heart beat wildly in her chest, she'd sweat heavily, and salivate profusely. Eventually her skin began to shed in layers.

Elizabeth stopped looking at the evidence of the illness

between her legs. The weeks passed. She drowsed as much as possible, yet found little satisfying deep sleep. Spots appeared on her skin, she had swollen, bleeding gums, severe aches in her joints, and bed sores. With time, she retreated into herself and no longer cared to understand the words of the patients, nurses, and physicians.

Elizabeth knew she would die. Indeed, she welcomed death. She hoped to go to heaven.

After what I did to the old woman, I am not worthy of such a reward, but perhaps God will not judge me too harshly. Even as the thoughts formed, she could not determine in her delirium if she truly believed in God and Heaven. Elizabeth was resigned to whatever might befall her.

A long period of grayness ensued.

The grayness began to lift. Elizabeth wasn't certain she wanted to emerge from herself. In moments of wakefulness, she squinted fearfully at the ward through half-shut eyelids. The treatments ceased and her symptoms began to fall away, one by one. She was feeling better, and when she could finally understand the nurses again, she was told that her chancre had spread dramatically before the course of the disease was reversed.

Elizabeth was discharged in late September. Although considered cured, she had continuing appointments and a responsibility to report the findings to the police.

When she returned home, her key fit the padlock on the door as before, but inside the room, she found someone else's clothing in the cabinet. Banked coals in the stove were keeping the room warm.

Exhausted after her walk from Kurhuset, she lay on the bed. The mattress had ceased to smell of rotting flesh.

Klaudio had no doubt had the room cleaned and given it to another of his prostitutes, yet he was too miserly to pay for a new padlock.

Sleep, Bess said. *Whoever she is, she will understand your need for rest.*

11

REST

Elizabeth was awakened by Ada. She was relieved to think that the room currently belonged to someone she knew.

Ada sat on the edge of the bed and gave Elizabeth a cup of coffee. "You've grown so thin. Are you hungry?"

"Yes," Elizabeth said.

Ada gave her bread. Elizabeth dunked it into her cup of coffee, took a bite and chewed. She'd never known coffee and bread to taste so good.

"I've a story to tell you, Elizabeth," Ada said, "a wonderful story."

Elizabeth was busy with her food and drink and not paying much attention to her friend's words.

"A woman came looking for you two weeks ago. I was leaving my room at the time. She asked after you, but I wasn't certain what I should tell her at first. When she asked if I worked for Klaus, I said I did. She said that she did too, and gave me her given name. She said she was Leena—"

Elizabeth looked up, instantly intent on Ada's words.

"—and that she had worked with you in a nearby household."

"Yes," Elizabeth said, eager to hear more.

"As we talked I could see she was a decent sort. I told her what had become of you and that we were friends. Because I visited Kurhuset frequently to find news of your wellbeing, I was able to tell her about your progress and that there was hope for your release soon."

Elizabeth was embarrassed. "What was her response?" she asked.

"She was sympathetic. She said that her employer, whose name she would not say, had been looking for you."

Fru Ellstromsdotter? Elizabeth wondered.

Perhaps to gloat over your suffering, Liza said.

Possibly, Herr Olovsson, Bess said.

"What would he want with me," Elizabeth wondered aloud.

"I have not spoken to your benefactor, the employer, I presume. Leena took away the news I offered." Ada paused and smiled before continuing. "Klaus came to me a few days later. He said I was to clean your room and help you when you returned from Kurhuset. He said I would not see clients for whatever length of time it took to bring you back to health. While I was cleaning the next day, he brought fresh clothing into your room."

She got up and moved to the cabinet. "It's all folded neatly in here." Ada picked up a letter off the cabinet and handed it to Elizabeth. "Then, this came for you yesterday."

The sender's name was Leena Jensson. Elizabeth tore the envelope open and read.

Dearest Elizabeth,

I hope this letter finds you feeling better. I am saddened to hear of your recent suffering. I did not know that Herr Lydersson kept women in such cruel circumstances until Herr Olovsson asked me if I knew if you were doing well, and I took it upon myself to find out for him. I have since disassociated myself from Herr Lydersson.

When I found out about your suffering, I was reluctant to tell Herr Olovsson about it for fear of revealing that which your pride might prefer to keep. But he is a good-hearted man, and I had a feeling he might be able to help since he was a policeman for many years and maintains connections within the city police.

And, indeed, he has been able to help. Herr Lydersson is now watched carefully. His women are to be protected.

When you are feeling well again, hopefully soon, Herr Olovsson has found possible employment for you with a German musician and his wife who have recently come to our city. They eagerly await a chance to meet with you. If you cannot come soon, and the opportunity passes, be assured that Herr Olovsson will make available further opportunities.

Of most importance is the task of regaining your health. When you're ready, write to me at my mother's address, 28 Timmer Mans Platsen.

Herr Olovsson said to tell you he misses your coffee.

My most fervent hopes for you,
Fru Leena Jensson

Tears fell from Elizabeth's eyes as she handed the letter to Ada. The older woman began to weep as she read. When she was done, she took Elizabeth in her arms, hugged her, and then stood.

"Rest," she said before leaving the room.

Elizabeth needed no further encouragement.

12

GOODWILL

Leena remained the go-between for Elizabeth and Herr Olovsson. She suggested that Elizabeth take a heritable name to create a separation from her record with the police. Out of respect for her family, Elizabeth was reluctant, yet finally she took the name Gustavsson, after the family name she'd given her stillborn girl since it was not so different from her Gustavsdotter.

In November of 1865, she gained employment within the household of the German musician Carl Kirschner, a violinist with the Gothenburg Grand Theatre. Although Elizabeth's income was slightly less than what she'd earned within the Olovsson household, she didn't mind. She had a room in the Kirschner home, was kept warm and well-fed. Herr Kirschner was in his mid-forties. He was thin and balding. His face was expressive and he spoke with a heavy German accent. His wife, Inga, a twenty-year-old aspiring actress, was quite beautiful, with long, curly, dark hair, a full mouth, large blue eyes, and rosy cheeks. Their home was in no way ostentatious, but the house had a large parlor for social events, and the couple held small parties frequently. They led exciting lives with their many friends from the theatre. The men and women who visited the house were charming and handsome, their clothing expensive, colorful, and stylish.

Fru Kirschner was studying English with the hope of expanding her potential on the stage, and Elizabeth was delighted to practice the use of the language with her. They spent many hours together, having conversations in both Swedish and English.

To be around such excitement and beauty, Bess said, *is certainly something better than the life of a prostitute.*

Elizabeth had survived a great ordeal and felt humbled, yet strengthened by the experience. She believed she knew the worth of life for the first time, and was eager to listen to her hopeful half. Liza had little to say, almost as if she were sleeping, and Bess's attitude came to the fore. *Never again must anger, melancholy, pettiness, complacency, and selfishness sully your days,* Bess suggested. *You can go forth and love life and all it has to offer with a childlike abandon.*

While skeptical that she could continue with the same rosy outlook, Elizabeth intuitively felt the truth of Bess's statements. She clung to her joy and the gratitude that went with it, knowing they were the key to maintaining the frame of mind.

Elizabeth knew happiness in the first week as she went about her duties, cooking, cleaning, and serving. In the time that followed, however, Liza Black Tongue slowly emerged from hibernation.

The first party in the Kirschner home at which Elizabeth served was held for ten or twelve guests. Elizabeth had been with the

Kirschners for about a month. As the evening wore on and the guests lounged in the parlor with liqueurs and brandy, the men were telling of the foolish things they'd done to impress women. Elizabeth stood beside the doorway to the hall and listened.

Following a humorous story told by a loud fat man with wild auburn hair, Herr Kirschner spoke up. "My story is not as funny," he said, glancing at his wife with a mischievous look, "but I'll tell it anyway. We were hiking in the Alps with the Ehrlich's, and Inga kept eyeing Hans's posterior."

Frau Kirschner blushed, and covered her mouth as she giggled. The guests shouted their approval.

"Although not normally the jealous sort, it came to me that I needed to regain Inga's attention by an act of physical strength. I decided to climb a rock face. I could have walked a small path to the top, which was some thirty feet up, but my intention was to amaze, to astonish!" Herr Kirschner held his thin arms out in a strongman pose.

The guests jeered in good humor while Frau Kirschner laughed.

I should not know such things about those I serve, Elizabeth decided. She slipped out the door to go to the kitchen to fetch more brandy. As she went, she heard intermittent laughter from the guests between the murmurs of Herr Kirschner's statements.

Upon her return, the tale seemed to be winding down. She moved about the room, offering more brandy to some of the guests whose glasses were almost empty.

"Inga had given me the fine jacket as a birthday present," Herr Kirschner said. "Looking much more heroic, Hans was able to lift me to safety. The jacket was ruined, torn against the rock."

"It was much more expensive than you deserved, anyway!" Inga shouted in mock-anger. She was drunk.

"Now, gentlemen," Her Kirschner said, standing and bowing slightly, "*that* is how to impress your woman."

The guests agreed with great guffaws.

Elizabeth decided she hadn't missed much. Looking at the

audience, she was certain the story was much better for the intoxicated listener.

They seem to think that because they're in the theatre, the things they say are entertaining, Liza said.

Elizabeth rejected the bitter thought. She liked the Kirschners. Their marriage was one of true love. They treated her with respect. She had been encouraged to feel comfortable enough to speak her mind within their household.

"You seemed a little uncomfortable last night, Elizabeth," Frau Kirschner said the day after the party.

"No, Frau Kirschner, not at all."

"Inga, please."

"Yes, Inga."

"During parties, though you are serving, you should relax and feel free to talk to the guests," Inga said. "As long as you don't have too much and become foolish or clumsy, you should have a drink."

"Thank you, Frau Kirschner—I mean, Inga," Elizabeth said, "but I don't care much for the way I act with drink."

"I understand about drinking. Some of us have difficulty. I should not drink as much as I do."

Elizabeth smiled shyly. In the short time she'd served in the household, she'd helped Inga to bed more than once when the woman had had too much to drink. The amount of drunkenness within the household was distressing at times. Elizabeth was alternately attracted to the drinking and repulsed by it. She hadn't had a drink in several years, and remembering the consequences from times past kept her from it.

With time, Inga offered up her history to Elizabeth as if to a close friend. Both she and her husband told more stories of their adventures and their rather tame improprieties. Elizabeth became uncomfortable with her own reticence and thought that she should express herself more. Perhaps she should tell them something of her past.

Yet she didn't have adventures that were daring and humorous. They would not want to hear about her prostitution, her bout with venereal disease, and the loss of her infant. Ultimately, she had trouble feeling worthy of their confidence and good graces.

Yes, excitement and beauty had come into Elizabeth's life, but she could only stand in the wings and watch. Her existential delight had been short-lived.

It seems that something better *has its limits*, Liza said.

Almost a month later, while Elizabeth was cooking dinner, Inga came to the kitchen to ask for a cup of coffee. "You make a most wonderful cup, my dear."

"I have heard that before, Inga. Thank you."

As the lady of the house sat at the big oak kitchen table, Elizabeth put a pot of water on the stove, measured out finely ground coffee from an earthenware jar with a wide cork in it, and dumped them in.

"Do you recall meeting Herr Godvin Bohlander last week?" Inga asked.

"Yes," Elizabeth said, "the handsome actor."

"Yes. Do you know that he kissed me in the hallway when no one was watching?"

Elizabeth didn't know what to say. She remained silent for a moment, then simply smiled.

"He wanted to take me to his bed," Inga said with a girlish giggle, "I wouldn't let him because I love my husband."

A question had been nagging at Elizabeth, and, remembering that she'd been invited to speak her mind, she spoke up. "Inga, you and Herr Kirschner are very good to me, but why do you treat me like such a good friend when you don't truly know me?"

"I hope I haven't shocked you," Inga said, a look of concern on her face.

"Not at all," Elizabeth said. "I have had experience with men." She looked for a new way to ask the question. "Customarily, those who have been hired to serve are not considered to be the friends of those they serve."

Inga's face became sad. "You're asking why we don't treat you as an inferior from a lower class."

Elizabeth nodded uncertainly, and Inga pinched her lips together as if the answer was difficult to formulate.

"Well, my husband is a follower of the writings of Karl Marx." She paused. "I don't understand all of it, but…we don't believe there should be separate classes. We don't believe some are better or worse than others. We think that…everyone should be treated equally."

Elizabeth didn't find an answer in what the woman had to say—not one that she understood—and it must have shown on her face.

Inga became flustered. She stood and approached. "Oh, you are so serious, my dear." She cupped Elizabeth's chin in one hand and smiled. The motherly gesture was more than a little uncomfortable for Elizabeth since she was two years the woman's senior.

She treats you like a little girl, even as she says you're equals, Liza said.

She's being affectionate, Bess said.

Elizabeth kept an even gaze.

"You are our servant," Inga continued. "You're *also* our friend." She laughed and rolled her eyes as she stepped back. "I don't tell about my dalliances to just anyone. I know you're not judging when you look at me. I can say *anything* to you!"

Elizabeth took the boiling pot from the stove, and poured the woman a cup of coffee.

"Thank you, dear," Inga said.

"What I meant to ask," Elizabeth said, "is why do you befriend *me* in particular." She regretted the question immediately.

"And why not?"

Elizabeth choked on her words. She didn't want to admit the truth—she didn't want to face it herself—but the lady of the house was still waiting for an answer. Finally Elizabeth decided to take a big risk. "I have done a terrible thing," she said quietly.

"Nonsense!" Inga waved her hand in the air as if she could dispel blame for the worst deeds with a simple gesture. "You're a charming person. We've all done things we regret." She smiled brightly, picked up her cup of coffee, and headed for the door to the hallway.

"What I did to Fru Andersdotter..." Elizabeth said.

The lady of the house gave no indication that she'd heard. She left the kitchen and moved down the hall.

Elizabeth felt abandoned. She would have opened up for the woman. Inga didn't take her seriously enough to want to listen, however. Elizabeth had lost her courage—she knew she would never bring the subject up again.

She doesn't want to know, and you shouldn't tell her, Liza said.

You can't blame her for not wanting to hear the worst, Bess said. *She wants to think the best of you. That's the way of friendship.*

A month later, as the year of 1865 was coming to a close, and Inga brought forth the news that she was expecting, Elizabeth found herself inexplicably wanting out of her employment. She had only been with the Kirschners for two months.

Am I so afraid of the alcohol, she asked herself, *or am I merely foolish and ungrateful again*?

You fear the newborn will remind you of your loss, Bess said.

You know that if you stay, you'll end up having to raise her whelp, Liza said cruelly.

Since Elizabeth was looking for reasons to escape the

Kirschner household, for a time she entertained the excuses provided by her two selves, although neither was at the heart of her desire to leave. She tried to tell herself that at the age of twenty-two, she didn't want to watch others go on about their lives while she merely served and had no life of her own. When that didn't fit, she tried out several more excuses, yet none of them stood up to scrutiny and the truth pressed in.

A few months earlier, when the wreck of Elizabeth's life was going down and she was drowning in a sea of misery, Herr Olovsson had thrown her the lifeline of employment with the Kirschners. She would not have met Herr Olovsson without Herr Rikhardsson's goodwill toward her. Herr Rikhardsson's trust in Elizabeth was in deference to Fru Andersdotter. If not for the friendship Hortense had had with members of Elizabeth's family on her mother's side, the old woman would not have taken her in. The unbroken lifeline of goodwill ran straight through the good hearts of those generous souls and all the way back to Fru Beata Carlsdotter. For all that, Elizabeth had frequently shown her mother little but tolerance.

If she could express her gratitude to her mother, Elizabeth might feel better, for it seemed the woman continued to look out for her, even from the grave. Lying in bed one night, she spoke to the darkness. "Thank you mother for all the many things you did to give me life. Thank you for protecting me and showing me the goodness in the world." She had no sense that anyone listened, however, and a nagging sense of unworthiness began to plague her.

If any of the people who had helped her knew what she'd done, they would be as horrified as was Elizabeth. In her worst moments, she considered herself Hortense's murderer. Elizabeth's weapon had been ingratitude and callous neglect. Along with those thoughts came the belief that she had indeed been rejected by her own infant daughter. In those moments, nothing Liza or Bess said would help her break free from the cycle of regret and recriminations that wound around and through her thoughts like a venomous snake ready to poison any good notions that might arise.

The kinder the Kirschners were to Elizabeth, the more wretched she felt. Her employment was a constant reminder of the goodwill she didn't deserve. She had to get away from them, and build a life of her own, if she was ever to feel worthy of happiness and friendship again.

If Inga were your friend, she'd have been willing to listen to your troubles, Liza said. *The Kirschners are theatre people. They want an audience for their drama. They treat you well because they want to be loved.*

In the future, when you have friends of your own, Bess said, *friends of* your *choosing, you won't be troubled. True friendship should bring you nothing but satisfaction and joy.*

Ada and Leena were my friends.

Ada and Leena are whores, Liza said. *You cannot expect people to offer you respect if you are friendly with prostitutes.*

I have been a prostitute.

Yes, Liza said. *You don't have to tell people about it, though. If you get to England, you'll leave your past behind.*

The last bit of advice seemed the only reasonable one. Elizabeth cultivated her dream of London, and the one about the coffee house Herr Olovsson had suggested, yet she couldn't see either in her future with the wages she earned.

On Christmas Day, 1865, she received a present from her father that she believed would make all that possible. After his sale of the family farm, Elizabeth's father sent her a share of what was earned. Once more, her mother was looking out for her from the grave—the farm had belonged to her, and was sold to her brother. And again, Elizabeth felt undeserving, but she did her best to set the feeling aside. The sixty-five Swedish Crowns would not last long. However, it would get her to London and hopefully give her a chance at a new life, at something better.

13

PASSAGE

Elizabeth presented to the Kirschners her exit from service as the beginning of a longed-for adventure to visit and begin life anew in London, England. The Kirschners saw her dream as a romantic notion well worth pursuit.

"I have a good friend who would serve you well in my stead," Elizabeth told the lady of the house. "Her name is Ada."

"I'll speak to my husband about it," Inga said. Shortly thereafter, Herr Kirschner asked Elizabeth to organize an interview with Ada.

Elizabeth didn't know if the woman would truly be suited for the job, but wanted to give her a chance to get away from prostitution. She visited Ada, and did her best to prepare her for the interview. Elizabeth made sure the woman was clean and wearing fresh, sober clothing. The most difficult aspect of the preparation was reminding Ada to hold her features in some semblance of hope. Elizabeth was satisfied with the results in the short term. She worried that the woman might not be able to maintain her appearance and manner for long. Still, she felt good about trying to help. The rest was up to Ada.

Herr Kirschner wrote to one of his friends, a British musician who played cello in the orchestra at the Standard Music Hall in London, a fellow named Lawrence Pimberton, to tell him about Elizabeth, and ask if she might be taken into his service with room and board. The answer came back that he had no immediate need, but that if she were to call on him at his home, he might find something for her. In any case, he was willing to pose as her employer to smooth her immigration, and provide her with lodging for a fortnight upon her arrival.

Elizabeth applied for and received her change of address certificate from the Church of Sweden. Herr Kirschner provided Elizabeth with a letter of introduction addressed to British Immigration, explaining his release of her service into that of Mr. Lawrence Pimberton at 30 Ledbury Road, London. Herr Kirschner took her to his bank to have her inheritance converted into British currency.

Elizabeth left for England on the Steamship Ahlberg on February 7, 1866. During the two and a half day passage across the North Sea, she rode on the between deck, just below the main deck of the ship. The area was cramped, with a six foot ceiling height. The bunks for the steerage passengers were temporary wooden structures built along the sides of the ship. She shared her bunk with four strangers. Her few possessions, packed into a recently purchased carpet bag, were stored under the bunk with the luggage of her bunkmates.

With the constant, slow pitching motion of the ship, Elizabeth was seasick and sleepless most of the voyage, and her bunkmates wanted nothing to do with her. She sat on the edge of the bunk and hung her head. Even if her nausea had allowed her to sleep, the rumbling and vibration of the steam engine would've made slumber difficult.

A young steward with a pocked face named Bilford provided her with a bucket in which to be sick. He stooped as he moved about the 'tween deck on his rounds, checking on the passengers and replacing the bucket with an empty one when needed. The steward was English, as was most of the crew.

No food was provided in steerage. Elizabeth had brought with her bread and cheese, but she hadn't had an appetite. The last sleepless night of the voyage, she spent sitting on the deck and leaning back against the structure of the bunk. She dragged her carpet bag out from under the bunk to use as a pillow and dozed fitfully.

One of her bunkmates climbed down to seek the privy and stepped on Elizabeth's left hand. No real damage was done. When the woman returned, she glared before climbing back into her bed. Elizabeth paid her no mind. As miserable as she was, she had hope for her future that kept her in good spirits.

Much later, she awoke as the rhythm of the engine changed. The pitching motion of the ship was greatly diminished, and Elizabeth felt no forward momentum.

A small, black, prick-eared dog approached in the dim light provided by the swaying lanterns. The animal sniffed her empty bucket.

"That's Perry," Bilford said in English. She hadn't heard the steward approach. "Thought you two might give each other some comfort."

When she frowned to show she didn't understand, he repeated himself in Swedish.

Elizabeth nodded. She was unenthusiastic. Perry nuzzled her hand until she lifted it and ran it across the top of his head and down his back.

The steward is after something more than light conversation, Liza said. *Otherwise, his time would be occupied with the needs of the first class passengers.*

His job among the steerage passengers is minimal, Bess said, *yet he's a friendly Englishman who takes pride in his work.*

"He's very insistent," Bilford said slowly in English. "He's a schipperke—means 'little skipper.' Perry is the captain's dog. He helps keep the ship clear of rats and mice."

The dog had only a nub for a tail. An extra thick ruff around his neck was a soft place for her fingers to explore, and Perry clearly enjoyed the petting.

"We've entered the Thames and await a river pilot," he said, "Once we're underway again, the passage will be smoother."

When the steward had gone, Perry remained. He curled up beside Elizabeth. The petting took her mind off her nausea and the dog kept her company until she fell into a light sleep. When she awoke with a sore backside, Perry was gone, and there was commotion on the main deck above. Men were shouting in English. She couldn't understand them because of their heavy accents. Early light spilled through the opening to the main deck. The sharp fish-rot-odor of a riverbank and raw sewage reached her nose. The rhythm of the engine was faster, but the pitching motion of the ship remained light.

The steerage passengers were up and around, checking their luggage and talking. Elizabeth felt several shudders run through the vessel as if it were bumping against a fixed object.

Bilford, stepped onto the 'tween deck. "Be prepared to disembark. You must wait until I've received the order from the captain before you can climb to the main deck," he said. "You will file before the customs and immigration officers who will meet you on the quay. We have arrived at the London Docks, and it shouldn't be more than a quarter of an hour wait."

Elizabeth was shaking, and she tried to tell herself that she did so in keen anticipation. Sitting on her carpet bag, she tried again to imagine what life would be like in London. The photographs she'd seen over the years had given her the barest glimpse, one that she didn't trust because the tintypes and daguerreotypes, mostly of famous landmarks, looked more like paintings in soot by artists with failing sight. Powerful, unpleasant odors, polluted air, the booming sounds of steam-powered machinery, and the distant rumbling of the city's bustling humanity were already discernible from the 'tween deck. She tried to shut it all out and imagine the shining city she'd seen in her mind's eye so many times, but the sounds and smells put her in mind of another notion, one of London as a hungry beast. The foul air was its breath, the stink rose from its filthy hide, and the sounds came from the lurching of its joints and the churning and grinding of its digestive system. Swallowed whole, the SS Ahlberg had slid down the snaking river-throat to the gut of the great metropolis. Soon Elizabeth would be ejected from the ship onto the streets to fend for herself within the body of the beast. She was afraid.

14

THE BEAST'S BELLY

Elizabeth offered Herr Kirschner's letter of introduction and her change of address certificate to the Customs and Immigration officers. The Customs officer was done with her quickly. Standing before the Immigration officer, she was required to fill out two forms and to sign both. Her hand shook as she did so. When the officer asked where she would be staying, she lied, saying that she intended to reside in the Swedish Parish of London because that was what her change of address certificate stated.

"That isn't near your employer," the officer said, pointing to the address in Herr Kirschner's letter.

"I will be staying in the home of my employer for now," Elizabeth said, "I hope to one day live in the Swedish Parish." Although she had no desire for such an eventuality, she would say anything that might end the interview.

The officer had a long face that betrayed no emotion. He looked at Elizabeth in silence for a moment. Her heart beat so powerfully in her chest that she feared he might somehow notice and become more suspicious. Instead, he nodded and returned her documents. Relieved, Elizabeth assumed that he didn't see her presence in his country as any sort of threat.

More to the point, Liza said, *they don't consider Sweden a threat.*

Elizabeth was allowed to walk away, and she didn't look back. She wished she'd asked for directions, but had wanted to appear to know what she was doing.

The docks were teeming with life and activity, cranes lifting cargo from ships, wagons drawn by giant draft horses maneuvering into position to receive cargo, coal deliveries for the steamships, victual and fresh water deliveries, porters pushing barrows, and a multitude of boys hurrying in all directions for various purposes. Dockworkers shouted to each other in order to be understood over the hubbub of voices that rose from those who milled about with less purpose, to be heard over the hiss of steam, the crash and rumble of heavy objects colliding, the creak and groan of rope and metal cable, the clomp of hooves and the shuffle of countless leather soles on paving stones.

The address for Mr. Pimberton was near Hyde Park, at 30 Ledbury Road. Elizabeth struggled to think about how to proceed while distracted by the sounding of a ship's whistle and those of slightly more distant trains, while startled by sudden laughter on her right and a cry of pain from one whose foot she'd trod upon. Struck by the elbow of a child blundering through the crowd, she felt a rising panic.

The London beast is trying to digest you, Liza said. *You must get out of the tumult, now!*

Elizabeth turned away from the water and pushed forward. The crowd gave way with little resistance. She would ask for directions when she found an area with less commotion. Keeping a firm grip on her carpet bag, she followed people moving with purpose along a lane between two massive stone and brick warehouses. Beyond the buildings, she crossed several sets of railway tracks, passed between more brick structures and came to a road full of wagon and carriage traffic. Her panic had subsided. She kept to the footway that ran alongside the southern edge of the thoroughfare, and approached a gentleman leaning against a brick wall reading a newspaper.

"Please sir," she said haltingly in English, her heart in her throat, "can you tell me where to find number thirty, Ledbury Road?"

"Swedish?" he asked with a Prussian accent.

"Yes," Elizabeth said, and he smiled. She took a deep breath and her fear diminished a bit.

"Five or more miles that way." He pointed west, then turned back to his newspaper.

He's very friendly, Bess said.

Elizabeth walked. The wintry day was quite chill. The sun was out, but the air was heavy with haze. As she breathed deeply, she felt a tightness in her chest. Taking shallower breaths helped to ease the tightness. Now that she was on land, her appetite had returned. She ate some of her bread and cheese.

The types of structures along the road varied dramatically, from dwellings—both houses and tenements—to industrial buildings and places of business—warehouses, factories and shops. Sometimes the lane afforded a footway and sometimes not. When there was not one, and the amount of traffic along the road frightened her, especially the fast-moving carriages, Elizabeth pressed up against a building and waited until the road was clearer.

She was excited to see the Tower of London—a famous structure she'd seen in a dark photograph—come into view on her left. Again, her fear diminished. *I am indeed in London.*

Yes, Bess said, *you have arrived in the place where your life can begin again, without the burdens of your past.*

Elizabeth negotiated streets running in a westerly direction, until she had traveled about half a mile. Then she asked for directions from a woman who had stepped out of a small stone building. The structure, perhaps a large kitchen of some sort, had numerous smoking chimney pots and smelled of pastry and broth. The woman had emerged with her arms full of parcels wrapped in newspaper and tied with string. She didn't immediately understand Elizabeth, but was friendly. When she seemed certain about what Elizabeth was asking, she pointed to the west.

The Clock Tower that Elizabeth knew rose above Westminster Palace, the seat of British government, came into view to the south and dropped away as she continued. Elizabeth passed along streets through good and bad neighborhoods. One rookery in particular was composed of wooden buildings in worse condition than any she'd ever seen; ones with partially collapsed roofs, with destruction from fire and rot, with broken windows and boarded-up doorways. Despite the damage, the structures were clearly still inhabited. Smoke rose from dangerously crooked chimney pots, holes in roofs or even windows. Clothes lines ran from window to window between the buildings. Items rested on windowsills. Voices could be heard in the interiors.

Smells of cooking cabbage and potatoes made her stomach growl. She considered eating more bread and cheese, but the foulness of horse dung and slops in the road, churned together by hoof and wheel and swarmed by flies, discouraged her appetite.

As she moved through the rookery, she became fearful of its slovenly inhabitants. Their clothing and their flesh spoke of disease and decay, yet their eyes did not. The women on the street were not unfriendly, although some looked at her with suspicion.

They are gently warning you off to protect their own, Bess said. *They would become friends if they got to know you.*

The men, mostly elderly, sitting on stoops, gave her appraising looks and tipped their hats. Elizabeth lost some of her fear as she continued.

Men, Liza said, *ever hopeful of finding a way under your skirt.*

A filthy small boy ran by, trying to pluck her carpet bag from her as he went. Her grip was too strong. He spun around as he was brought up short, and almost fell. Several more small, raggedy boys across the road shouted insults at him. A woman sweeping soot from a doorway paused and shouted something angrily at the little thief. The boy turned his dirty face to Elizabeth and gave her a crooked grin full of good humor. The expression seemed to say, "Yes, you're tough enough for London."

Elizabeth smiled. He nodded to her and ran to join the other boys. They laughed and poked at him playfully.

They're having fun, Bess said. *What happy people Londoners are.*

They might be having fun, Elizabeth thought, *but as thin as they are, they must be hungry.*

She asked for directions several more times as she walked. Only one person turned her away rudely. Within a short time, she was confident of the route to take. Walking along Oxford Street, she came to the northern edge of Hyde Park. Looking through the leafless trees along the edge, Elizabeth saw lawns with manicured paths. She imagined how beautiful and green the park would become in springtime. The street had changed its name to Bayswater Road. She followed it west beyond the park to Pennbridge Gardens, where she turned right. Past a small garden square full of dormant trees and withered plants, she turned left at Ledbury Road and eventually found a tiny house with two doors. One was number 30, the door on the right, and the other was number 30 1/2, on the left.

Elizabeth knocked and waited, but no one answered.

The long walk and recent lack of sleep had left her exhausted. Her feet hurt. She sat on the stairs that led to the door of number 30, and rested her head against an upright for the railing. She was relieved to put down her bag. Her left hand, which had done the bulk of the carrying, was sore. She wrung the pain out of it with a few shakes.

Elizabeth would have to wait for Mr. Pimberton to come

home. She knew from his correspondence with Herr Kirschner that he worked on Friday evenings, going in after supper. Looking at the position of the sun overhead, she estimated that the time was three or four o'clock in the afternoon. Had she missed him? If so, night would descend and the temperature would drop as she waited.

You are tired out, Liza said. *If you wait here and fall asleep, you might not awaken. If the temperature plummets or ruffians find you, you're as good as dead.*

Elizabeth was too exhausted to listen to Liza. Mr. Pimberton was expected to be staying at his home that night, so he would eventually appear. If need be, she'd open her bag and don extra clothing. The neighborhood was a moderately good one, and she decided she had little to fear.

Elizabeth propped herself against the railing as best she could and closed her eyes.

The London beast had not succeeded in digesting her—not yet.

15

THE BEAST TAMED

Elizabeth was roused from her slumber by a plump man of about thirty years of age in a plaid suit. He had a round face and a bulbous nose, green eyes and a full head of light brown hair under a round brown felt hat. Perhaps assuming she was a vagrant, he was in the process of shooing her away from his front door, even as she became aware of him. He wasn't particularly aggressive, and she was trying to ignore him when she realized who he was.

"Mr. Pimberton?" she asked, frowning.

He became still and his head tilted slightly as if he were trying to recall something. Finally, he said, "I'm so sorry, you're Miss Gustavsson, aren't you?"

Elizabeth nodded and hugged herself. Night had come and the air was much colder.

"I had forgotten you were to come today."

She was still not entirely awake as he helped her to stand,

lifted her bag, ushered her into his small home, and shut the door. She stood still for a moment while he fumbled in the dark and finally lit a lamp which he set on an end table beside a settee.

"A pleasure to meet you, sir," Elizabeth said. She was shivering.

"Please call me Larry." He handed her the carpet bag.

"Yes, Larry," she said, despite discomfort using his first name.

"I'll get you a blanket to help you warm up." He walked into the next room, leaving the door open. He lit another lamp, opened a trunk and rummaged within.

The place appeared to have two rooms. The air inside was nearly as chill as that outside. She could see a small stove against the far wall of the next room.

Mr. Pimberton returned with a brown wool blanket and handed it to her. She set her bag down and wrapped the blanket around her shoulders.

"I'll light a fire," he said, and moved into the next room to the stove.

Elizabeth could see clothing strewn about both chambers. In the room she occupied, liquor and wine bottles were discarded in the corners. A half-eaten meal of fried fish in its paper wrapper sat beside the lamp on the end table.

When finished lighting the stove, Mr. Pimberton returned. He appeared to notice the fish for the first time, and snatched it up off the end table, disturbing several flies. They buzzed in circles about him as he carried the unfinished meal to a rubbish bin. Once he'd tossed the fish in and replaced the lid on the bin, he turned to Elizabeth looking rather embarrassed. She was pleased to find him not the least bit threatening. Still, she stood with the blanket draped over her shoulders, not knowing how to react.

"I'm not here much of the time," he said. "But clearly I need help keeping the place clean, and it would be better to return home in the winter months to a warm chamber. I can only afford to pay you one shilling per day, half of what you're worth. That's better than no job at all, I suppose, while you look for something better. You can sleep in the parlor tonight." He gestured toward the settee. "Tomorrow, we can clear out the room next door, and you could make it your own so the neighbors won't talk." He raised his eyebrows comically to indicate that he thought such talk was foolishness. "I take all my meals out. Well—" He glanced at the rubbish bin. "—most of them." He raised his eyebrows in a questioning look. "What do you say?"

"Yes," she said, nodding her head, "Until I find other work, I'd be pleased to have the job." She used her right foot to push her bag between the legs of the end table. Then, she began to move about, straightening the room.

"Miss Gustavsson," Mr. Pimberton said, "I'm sure you're exhausted from your travels. The housekeeping can wait. Please rest. Make yourself comfortable on the settee and put your feet up. I'll get you a pillow. Tomorrow isn't far away."

Elizabeth abandoned her work and gratefully accepted a small pillow. "Thank you, sir," she said with a smile.

Over the last few years, she'd become unabashed about exposing her body to men. She wanted to leave that life behind, and had no intention of testing his sensibilities. "I'll sleep in my clothing, Mr. Pimberton."

"As you wish, Miss Gustavsson," he said, waving his hand dismissively, "but I'm not concerned with such decorum, and I am no threat to you."

Elizabeth nodded. She noted that he didn't again insist she use his first name.

Perhaps he is a perderast, Liza said.

"In the morning then," he said.

As Mr. Pimberton took up a book and moved through the door to the next room, Elizabeth said, "Goodnight."

"Goodnight, Miss Gustavsson." He shut the door behind him.

Elizabeth remained chilled to the bone, and was concerned that the warmth from the stove wouldn't reach her until she saw that the fanlight above the door to Mr. Pimberton's room was open. She reclined on the settee and pulled the blanket over her. The cushions and the blanket warmed with time, and her chill went away. Finally, she was able to relax, and the day's tensions, stored in her frame, were released.

When Elizabeth awoke in the late morning, Mr. Pimberton was gone. The settee had been a tolerable bed. The room was still warm.

On the end table, she found two keys, a silver coin with leaves and a crown on one side and a woman's head on the other, and a note, resting in a residue of oil from the fried fish.

Miss Gustavsson, thank you for your assistance. I hope you slept well. Here is a key to the lock on the door, one for the room next door, and payment for your first day of charring. I didn't want to disturb you, so I cleaned up the room next door, 30 1/2, while you slept. The work might not be to your standards, and for that I apologize. There is a tin of biscuits in my room, and you are welcome to them. Again, I will be in late, around 10 o'clock.

Elizabeth pocketed the keys and the coin.

Mr. Pimberton is a good man, Bess said.

Elizabeth could not continue in his service for long or she'd spend her inheritance keeping herself fed, but the situation would help. Her first goal was to investigate her new world to see what it offered and what that would cost her.

She located the privy behind the house and relieved herself. As she was returning, she discovered a well pump from which to draw water and a clothes line that ran from a rear window to the fence behind the privy.

Returning to the front of the house, she located the key to the lock on the door marked 30 1/2. She opened the padlock, took it from its hasp and opened the door. The room inside was dusty and largely empty. In one corner Mr. Pimberton had left a couple of music stands and a battered cello case. At the far end of the room was a small fireplace. Against the interior wall was a rope bed with a straw mattress. Her employer had put fresh linens and a heavy wool blanket on it. Making the room livable looked to be quite possible.

Elizabeth left the room, put the lock on the door, and returned to the other side of the house. She ate some of her bread and cheese as she looked around. In Mr. Pimberton's room, she found a pitcher, a basin, a wash tub, and soap. The heating stove against the rear wall had a small surface for cooking and a reservoir for making hot water. The exhaust pipe was routed up the room's small chimney flue.

Finished eating, Elizabeth loaded the clothing scattered on the floor into the tub with some warm water. While the garments soaked, she worked on cleaning. She found no broom and did her best to sweep up using a newspaper that was a month out of date. Within a short time, she'd done what she could for the house and turned to the laundry. Mr. Pimberton lived in humble circumstances, but had clothing of good quality. Elizabeth was relieved to think that taking her on might not be such a hardship for him.

With the laundry done and hung to dry, she left the house, locking the door behind her. She asked the first person she met on the street where she could shop for meats and vegetables, and was directed to the Portobello Road Market, less than half a mile away. Once there, she found meat and vegetables being sold from outdoor stalls and costermongers' barrows. Among the establishments along the road, she found one selling readymade clothing, a bakery, a tavern, and a chandler's shop, where she bought a broom. Merchants with barrows and those within the shops competed for attention, each shouting about their products and prices, some making a song or rhyme with their words. As Elizabeth strolled along the lane with others browsing the market, she saw various buskers along the street, singing, playing musical instruments, dancing or executing acrobatic feats. Some of them wore colorful costumes, others were more humbly dressed. Each employed a boy carrying a small vessel, such as a cup. The boys asked for contributions from any who happened by. Beggars held their own cups tightly, and told their tales of woe.

Elizabeth saw children, girls and boys, lurking in the shadows, their feral eyes casting about for opportunities. Occasionally one would dash out quietly, brush past someone, and then disappear quickly. If one of the urchins came too close to a costermonger's or shopkeeper's goods, they were warned off. When she looked such a youngster in the eye, the child looked away quickly.

If they come after me, I have the broom to fend them off.

The guttersnipes are not interested in you, Liza said. *They can see you're not an easy mark.*

Or they see I have little of worth to steal, Elizabeth thought. She had almost brought her carpet bag with her when leaving Mr. Pimberton's house, and was glad she hadn't.

As she returned the way she'd come, the spring in Elizabeth's step was a hopeful one. Within a short time, she had found much of what she'd need to survive. Considering the prices she had encountered at market, she felt greater urgency to seek fuller employment, but was confident that could be achieved. Yes, she decided, she could live in London, and quite possibly thrive. She was certain that something better was well within her grasp.

You have been liberated from your past, Bess said.

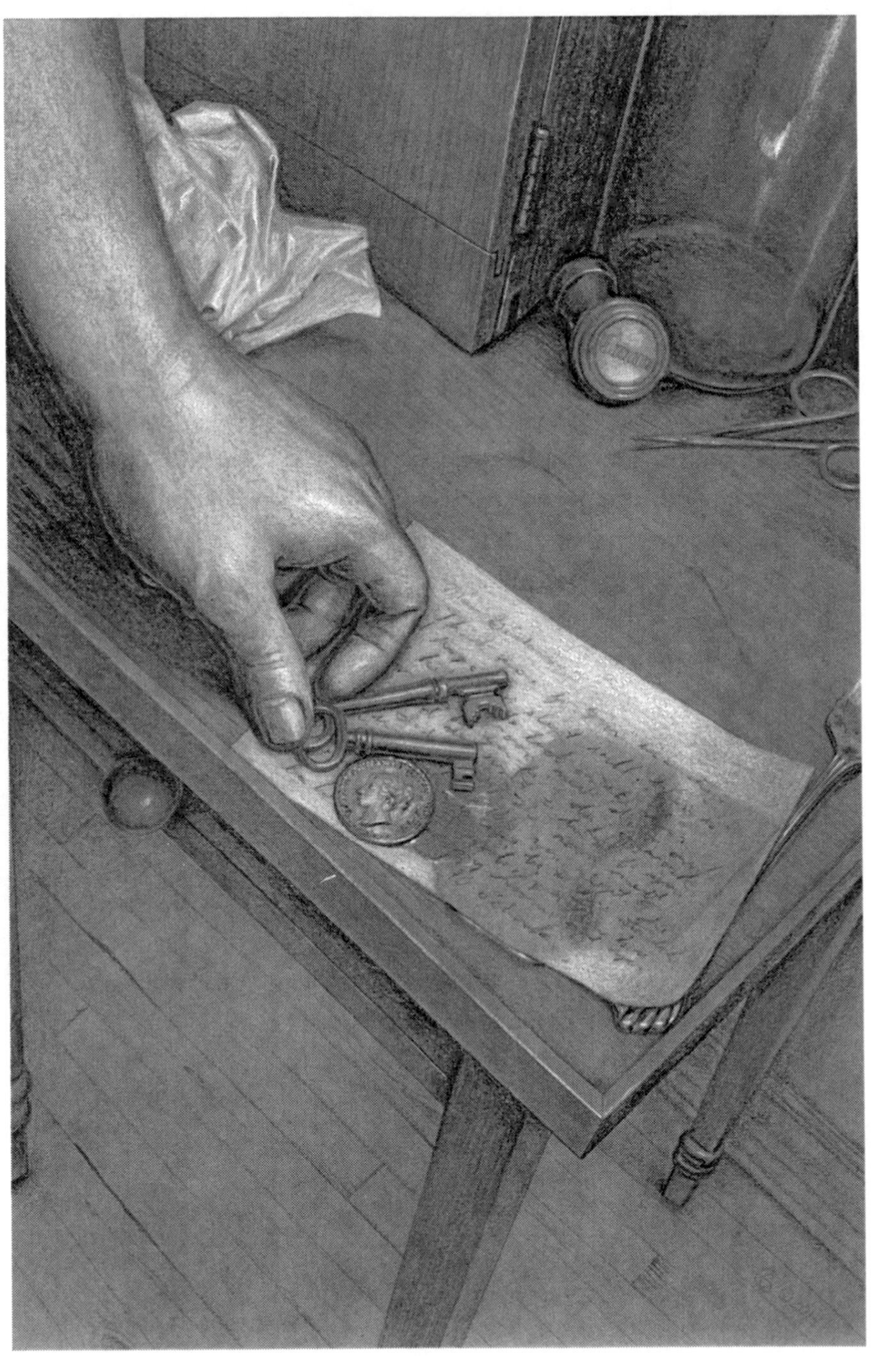

16

THE GUARDED SECRET

In the following months, Elizabeth's inheritance diminished slightly as she dipped into it to supplement her income. The majority of expense came early, as she outfitted her new room, and bought a few things at the Portobello Road Market to make her life more comfortable; cutlery, a cup, a bowl, a plate, a dutch oven for cooking, a few articles of clothing, a flannel, a towel, and a pillow for her bed.

She wrote to her father at the address he'd given her when he'd sent her inheritance, but she didn't expect an answer. He was her only connection to the place of her birth, however, and she didn't want to lose that. The correspondence was the beginning of a habit of writing to her father once a month.

One day, at market, she met a woman who looked remarkably like herself. The two were considering potatoes at a costermonger's barrow.

"You could be my twin sister," the woman said.

The voice belonged to one who was about Elizabeth's height, had a like shade of brown, somewhat curly hair, a long neck, grey eyes, and similar facial features.

"Yes," Elizabeth said, smiling. "You're quite pretty!" Her smile turned to a mischievous grin.

"Ah, that's how our mother would've told us apart," the woman said. "Your speech tells me you're from a distant land."

"Yes, from far away," Elizabeth said. "I'm Elizabeth, from Sweden."

"We are more twin than I thought," the woman said, laughing. "I am Elizabeth from England!"

After further introductions, the two women had a ploughman's lunch together at the Windsor Castle Pub. A market day for farmers selling livestock, the area that was partitioned off for the lower class was full of men drinking and talking about their successes or failures at auction. The two Elizabeths were the only women in evidence. Following suggestive remarks and ogling by some of the men, they were left to themselves.

In discussing their lives, Elizabeth held back what she considered unflattering about herself. She told of her early life on the farm in Torslanda, her service with families in Gothenburg, her desire to see London, and her experiences since.

"I come from Bath," the English woman said. "I have two children with my husband, William Watts. He's in America, seeing to property belonging to his family."

Elizabeth smiled, picturing the woman's children as looking something like Fru Ellstromsdotter's little ones.

Her new friend was quiet for a time, then she said, "I think your hands are bigger than mine." She held up her right hand. "Put yours against mine," she said. Her hand was chapped so badly, the joints of the fingers were cracked and scabbed over.

Elizabeth did as she was asked. She didn't want to touch the chapped skin, but didn't pull away as the English woman touched her.

"Your fingers are longer," the woman said. "You are Long Liz, then, and I must be Short Liz."

"Ah, that's another way our mother can tell us apart," Long Liz said. "She measures our fingers to decide which of us deserves punishment for stealing the jam."

The English woman laughed, her face crinkling up at the corners much the way Elizabeth's did when she laughed.

"I would be pleased if you would call me Lettie. That's what William calls me and I miss it."

"All right, Lettie," Elizabeth said.

As the conversation continued, it seemed her image in a mirror had taken on a life of its own. She liked that life, but to look upon the woman's hands pained her. Lettie used many hand gestures as she spoke. After a while, Elizabeth could take it no longer. She took Lettie's hands into her own. "Your fingers must hurt..."

"A little. I work for an elderly woman, Mrs. Huntermoon, in Ledbury Road," the English woman said. "I must scrub her kitchen floor every day. She believes rot is a demon. She calls him Eriot, and says he hides between the floorboards." Her smile was full of contempt. "If I wear him down enough, she says, he'll spend his time healing instead of doing more mischief in the kitchen."

"Again, we're twins," Elizabeth said, glad to have something to divert the conversation—she did not like remembering what it was like to work for an unreasonable employer. "I work for a *gentleman,* Mr. Pimberton, in Ledbury Road."

Lettie grinned. "Perhaps we'll be seeing a lot more of each other, Long Liz."

"I hope so," Elizabeth said as they parted company.

The next time she saw Lettie at the market, she invited her to take an excursion on the underground railway. "I will have at least one great adventure in my life," Elizabeth told her friend. Lettie accepted and they met the following morning at Paddington Station. Elizabeth paid three pence for each of them to ride to Farringdon Station—a distance of about four miles—and the same to ride back again. Sitting on a hard bench crowded with other passengers, they rode in one of several gas-lit third class wooden carriages drawn by a steam-powered locomotive. Pulling out of Paddington Station the carriage moved slowly, but by the time they passed underground Elizabeth was traveling faster than ever before in her life. Although she had no frame of reference, she had a sense that her speed was even greater in the darkness of the tunnel. The smoke within the underground passage was almost unbearable. The ride was so loud, the two women couldn't hear each other well enough to have a conversation. Still, Elizabeth was so thrilled she couldn't tell what was vibration from the carriage and what was her own excited quaking. Lettie grinned as she held Elizabeth's hands, and squeezed them when startled by loud sounds and sudden movements of the carriage.

On the return journey to Paddington Station, the steam engine was pushing the carriages instead of pulling them, and the air within the compartment was more breathable. The flame within the gas lamp fixture on the lefthand wall flickered and went out. In the darkness, Elizabeth felt herself merge with her twin and could no longer feel her friend's hands. Briefly, she had the notion that she'd always merely imagined Lettie. The woman no longer seemed to sit beside her and Elizabeth felt terribly alone. She had had few friends in life and dreaded the loss of companionship if Lettie were somehow gone. The strange feeling built toward panic until a gentleman passenger relit the gas lamp and Elizabeth saw her twin beside her again.

Lettie was a mirror of Elizabeth's own delight. They both suffered sore throats and coughing fits, yet the new experience was worth the discomfort. When the carriage slowed, a smell of burning wood entered the compartment.

The gentleman who'd lit the lamp must have seen the worried look on Elizabeth's face. "That's just the smell of the brakes," he said.

"Thank you, Long Liz!" Lettie said when they disembarked at Paddington Station. "I will not do that again soon—" She paused to bend forward and cough, then drew herself back up and grinned. "I'll need time to recover. But what a lark!"

"They say that one day the trains will be electric and there will be no s—" Elizabeth's words were cut off by her own hacking fit. Lettie patted her on the back and laughed. "—smoke," Elizabeth continued when she'd recovered. "The tunnels will be lit with electric lights and the lines will run everywhere in the city."

"Perhaps I'll wait until then to ride again," Lettie said with a playful grimace.

Elizabeth nodded in agreement.

She had luncheon again with Lettie at the Windsor Castle Pub the following Saturday.

Her new friend looked weary.

"It must be difficult working for Mrs. Huntermoon all day, while raising your children without their father," Elizabeth said.

"I couldn't have my children and work for Mrs. Huntermoon," Lettie said. "I haven't seen my little ones since shortly after William left for America. I don't know what's become of them." She had a grim smile.

"How can you not know?" Elizabeth asked, uncertain that she wanted to hear the answer.

"I come from a poor family. William does not. We fell in love and stole away to be married." The English Elizabeth smiled briefly, then her expression became grim again. "His family and friends didn't approve of our marriage. William's father sent him to America to separate us. Once he'd gone, William's friends took my children and sent them away. Someone got a physician to certify me insane. My own sister, Mary, helped them do it. I was locked up at the Fisherton House Asylum near Salisbury. It's a private madhouse. They earn for each person they keep. Getting released was difficult. The relieving office in Bath helped to get me out of the asylum, and I've worked as a domestic servant since. I hope to find my children one day. I've heard they might be in New Zealand, living with one of my husband's sisters."

Elizabeth was reminded of her time at Kurhuset, of her own pain and loss. "That's horrible." She took her friend's rough, chapped hands in her own.

"They would be two and three now, a boy, William, and a girl, Clara." Sniffling, Lettie took her hands away and wiped her face.

"I lost a child, a girl," Elizabeth said. Then she shook her head dismissively, "No, a stillbirth—it's not the same."

"Yet I see it hurts all the same," her friend said.

Elizabeth wanted to say more, but hesitated. Lettie had freely admitted that she had been in a lunatic asylum. In doing so, she'd shown no shame, and had trusted Elizabeth to understand and not judge too harshly. The English woman's face was open in a way that invited Elizabeth in. Her troubles wanted out. She had kept them to herself for too long, guarding them against exposure to judgment. In doing so, in only allowing Bess and Liza to reflect on her past, she had the sense that the truth of her own history was lost. Perhaps some of that truth could be recovered if she told her story to someone she trusted.

"I've done terrible things in my life," Elizabeth said.

Lettie didn't shrink away, so Elizabeth continued. She spoke for half an hour, long after they had finished eating, telling about her experience with Klaudio. The kindliness of Lettie's features didn't waver.

Finally, the publican approached, "If you please," he said, "have more or kindly leave." Despite his language, his words were not a request.

Lettie took Elizabeth's arm as they left the pub. "Let's walk through Hyde Park together."

Emboldened by her friend's acceptance, Elizabeth spoke about her time as a prostitute. Concerned with how her words were received, she turned to her twin often to look her in the eyes.

"I've thought of doing the same during hard times," Lettie said.

The two women made a circuit around Hyde Park as they talked. Spring had come and the flower beds were colorful. The lawns were dotted with picnicking couples and a few families. Playing children ran and tumbled. Men and women of higher classes strolled slowly along the paths as if they wanted to provide ample opportunity for others to see their fine clothing.

If only they could hear you, Liza said, *they would hound you out of the park.*

Lettie's acceptance suggests that people are less judgmental than you've believed them to be, Bess said.

Elizabeth told Lettie of her bout with venereal disease, about regrets for her ingratitude toward her mother.

"I too treated my mother poorly," Lettie said. "She told me that marrying above my station would only bring me heartache. I pretended she was jealous of my happiness. I told her that I knew she'd had a loveless marriage to my father and how cruel that had been for him, even though I knew nothing of the kind. He was gone by then and couldn't speak for himself. My mother and I didn't talk after that. Now she's gone too."

When they arrived at 30 1/2 Ledbury Road, Lettie hugged Elizabeth. "You truly are my sister, Long Liz," she said.

"Yes," Elizabeth said. She felt the need to say more, but what?

Lettie will become a loving friend if you let her, Bess said. *Tell her about what happened with the old woman. You need to get it off your chest.*

Elizabeth opened her mouth to do as Bess suggested. Lettie seemed poised to hear and accept more of Elizabeth's history.

Don't tell her, Liza said.

I made a mistake long ago, Elizabeth thought, *but that was all it was. If I can talk about it, perhaps I can find a way to forgive myself.*

No, Liza said, *she would know your inability to care for others, the weakness of your loyalty, your unfitness for love. Don't reveal that to her. She won't want to be your friend any longer.*

Shame washed over Elizabeth in a wave that sent her mind tumbling. Her heart turned sickeningly in her chest with the memory of discovering on the same day, so long ago, that she was a prostitute, that she was a drunk, and that she was a murderer. Despite knowing that what Liza suggested wasn't true, Elizabeth feared she must bear the burden of that terrible day alone to the grave.

"You were about to say?" Lettie said. "Something more troubles you?"

How does she know? Elizabeth wondered.

"No," she said, "not just now."

"You'll tell me when you're ready."

Give it time, Bess said.

Once Lettie had left her, Elizabeth expected she should feel somewhat unburdened. As she unlocked the door and entered her room, she knew that her lack of relief was due to her unwillingness to talk about what happened with the old woman.

You cannot trust anyone with that tale, Liza said.

In the following months Elizabeth saw her new friend frequently, especially on Saturdays at market. They ate luncheon together at the Windsor Castle Pub many times. The more time she spent with Lettie, the closer they became, and yet Elizabeth continued to guard her secret.

17

NO DIRTY PUZZLE

Mr. Pimberton introduced Elizabeth to several of his friends who were looking for help, but none could offer her a better situation than what she already had. By mid-July, fearing that she might be destined to run out her inheritance, become impoverished, and need help getting by, she decided to register at the Swedish Church.

Mr. Pimberton brought a friend to the house on a Sunday around noon in the winter of 1866. He knocked on her door and called out to her. Elizabeth was reclined on her bed, practicing her reading of English with a book her employer had lent her, one by George Eliot titled *Silas Marner*.

"Yes," Elizabeth said, as she opened the door. "I'm here, Mr. Pimberton." She recognized his voice, although the figures that stood before her were merely silhouettes against the bright and hazy, smoke-charged air outside.

"Miss Gustavsson," Mr. Pimberton said, "this is Police

Constable Winders. He's a good friend."

"Mr. Edward Winders, Miss," the constable said.

Elizabeth was embarrassed to be caught lounging with a book, even though she was not expected to work on a Sunday. "A pleasure to meet you, sir."

"And you, Miss Gustavsson," PC Winders said with a smile.

"Please come in." She stepped back and allowed the gentlemen to enter. Once inside, they stood awkwardly with no place to sit.

"He says he's looking for a housekeeper," Mr. Pimberton said.

As the constable looked around Elizabeth's chamber, she assumed he was assessing her work. She'd done her best with the room, having cleaned it thoroughly and put up a curtain over its one window. Mr. Pimberton had offered her a moth-eaten Persian rug that had been rolled up under his bed. She'd repaired a hole in it with heavy yarn and put it down on her floor to help lessen the chill that rose from beneath the house in cold weather. She'd gained few possessions, however, in the nine months she'd been in London.

As Mr. Winders looked around, Elizabeth was busy assessing him. At present, his figure and features were lit by the filtered light from the window instead of the glare of the hazy sky outside. He wasn't exactly handsome, yet something about his appearance in the constable uniform and his bearing made her heart beat faster.

"Well, I will leave you two to discuss business," Mr. Pimberton said, and he walked out and closed the door.

Not for the first time, Elizabeth wondered if he was eager to be rid of her. He had been nothing but pleasant, and she worked hard for her money. Still, the understanding they shared was that Elizabeth's employment was to be a temporary situation. She was certain he'd find another way to spend his money if she were gone.

"I *am* looking for a charwoman," Mr. Winders said, "though I suspect there's more to you than that." Without seeming excessively proud, he smiled as if he knew he'd made her heart beat faster. "Would you care to take a meal at the Barley Mow with me?"

Elizabeth smiled, and covered her mouth. She was taken by surprise and flattered.

He's taken an interest in you, Bess said.

Yes, Liza agreed, *you should be careful.*

Mr. Winders raised his eyebrows and tilted his head. The expression was so like that of an enthusiastic boy that Elizabeth became excited.

"Yes," she said.

He grinned. "Well, then, I will be back with a cab about half past three."

After he had gone, Elizabeth tried to settle down with her book again. She was too excited to read.

Having hired a hansom cab, Mr. Winders came for Elizabeth at the appointed time. Instead of his uniform, he was wearing a short tweed coat and brown trousers. Elizabeth donned her coat and bonnet and left her room, locking the door behind her. He helped her up into the cab, and when he was situated, he said, "Thank you, Harry." She presumed he spoke to the driver, as the vehicle began to move.

Elizabeth had rarely ridden in a carriage, and never in such a fine one. The front was open and she had a clear view through the windows to either side. The large wheels made for a relatively smooth ride over both the large and small granite paving stones, but was most quiet on the roads paved with wooden blocks.

Elizabeth considered the ride an extravagance meant to impress, and Mr. Winders seemed to anticipate her reaction. "Harry is my cousin," he said, jerking his thumb back toward the driver. "He charges me half-fare."

The constable had secured a drinking box for their meal at the Barley Mow Tavern. The small booth was relatively quiet and provided privacy. He ordered a dish of meat and vegetables to share and tall glasses of ale for each of them.

He wants to get you drunk so he can take advantage of you, Liza said.

Although Elizabeth listened to her cynical voice, she was comfortable with Mr. Winders. Still, she didn't drink her ale.

"Larry says you come from Sweden."

"Yes, I'm from Torslanda."

"That's near Gothenburg?"

"Yes." Elizabeth was terse as she busied herself eating gobs of fat from the joint they'd been served.

Mr. Winders was eating chunks of potato. "How did you happen to come to London?"

"I wanted to see the sights, and live in the grandest city in the world." Thinking she sounded like a child, Elizabeth blushed with a demure smile.

"And your family?"

"They're all in Sweden. I didn't want to live my life on a farm."

"Such a brave woman, to come all this way alone!" He seemed genuinely impressed. "We have something in common, then."

Elizabeth smirked playfully as she thought he meant that he, too, was brave.

"No, I meant that I didn't want a life on the farm. My father was a tenant farmer. We never had anything. I left my family behind and came to London to make a better life for myself. And I have." He looked handsome when he showed his pride.

"Then you are at least as brave as I am." Elizabeth gave him a coy smile.

When the constable reached over and wiped a bit of grease from her chin, she didn't pull away. Encouraged, he leaned in and kissed her on the mouth, then sat back and resumed his meal.

Elizabeth was delighted with his casual manner and light

touch. He didn't paw at her the way men had in the past. She got the impression that he was willing to see how their rapport developed before asking for more.

As their talk resumed, she noted that the conversation had a natural flow that she enjoyed, despite her occasional misunderstandings. Although her English had become much better within the time she'd lived in London, her slight difficulty with the language prompted her to ask him to explain a few things that might have been obvious to another.

With time, Elizabeth became full and stopped eating. Mr. Winders devoured what was left of the meat and vegetables. Sleepy after the heavy meal, she offered less to the conversation and sat listening as he talked.

"Until recently, my beat was along Brewer Street in Agar Town, not far from here," he said, "but it's been demolished as part of the site of the new rail station. For now, I patrol parts of the construction area. It's interesting, and there's some danger as so many were put out and their homes destroyed. Some come back again and again, even though there's nothing left for them there. There are those who say we are well-rid of Agar Town, that it was a breeding ground for the worst poverty and neglect, yet I knew many who lived there who did well, proud families of character."

The constable paused to finish his ale, and he looked at Elizabeth's glass. "You don't like ale?" he asked.

"I've never had ale."

"Oh, you must try it."

"I don't want to become drunken," she said, trying to be honest.

"Ale isn't that strong. Please try it."

See, Liza said, *he wants you drunk.*

When Elizabeth hesitated he smiled and nodded encouragement.

He wants you to enjoy yourself, Bess said. *He's not like other men.*

Finally, Elizabeth took up the glass and smelled the liquid. The odor of alcohol coming from the ale wasn't nearly as strong as she'd expected. She took a sip, and found the drink delicious. Sipping slowly, she came wide awake, and their conversation continued. She was relaxed and her warm feeling toward the man grew, but she didn't become intoxicated. While she immediately craved more when she finished her glass of ale, she was so distracted and taken with the gentleman beside her, she let the desire go.

When finally he took her to her home, she kissed him and invited him in. Mr. Winders considered the invitation for a moment, then paid the fare and dismissed the hansom cab. Elizabeth saw that the driver was not his cousin, Harry, and knew the ride must have cost him dearly.

She let them into her room. He moved to the fireplace, unbanked the coals that still smoldered and stoked the fire. Elizabeth sat on the floor beside him as he worked.

When he was done, he turned and held her and kissed her more passionately than before. As the room warmed, so did their passion. Finally they took to her small bed.

Elizabeth had not experienced anyone desiring her in the way Edward did. He seemed hungry for her, yet he was attentive to her needs. She was no dirty puzzle, and he was no desperate toad or vindictive cuckold. No, their intimacy was something better. For the first time, Elizabeth experienced sexual intercourse as a tender, loving act.

18

THE TERMS OF AGREEMENT

"I don't want to accept Mr. Winders's offer," Elizabeth told Lettie. They were having another ploughman's lunch at the Windsor Castle Pub in May of 1867. "To be intimate with him while in his service as a charwoman is prostitution, even if I do live under his roof. I don't want to be a whore anymore."

"Well, you're certainly good at rhymes," Lettie said with a crooked smile.

Elizabeth looked away, exasperated. She was trying to make an important decision.

She took a sip of her ale. Since being introduced to the drink, she'd had a glass of the brew at each of their luncheons.

When Mr. Winders had made the offer, he and Elizabeth had not spoken of his need for a charwoman since the night they began courting, six months earlier. She would earn half again what she earned working for Mr. Pimberton—not quite a living wage, but her inheritance would dwindle slower.

Bess, ever hopeful, had advised Elizabeth to do whatever the constable wanted. *If you make him happy enough, he will ask you to become his wife.*

If you live with him, Liza warned, *he'll no longer have to seek your company. He'll lose gratitude and tire of you.*

"You always say you want *something better,*" Lettie said, "Well, *here* it is. *I* think it sounds good." She had followed Elizabeth's affair with Mr. Winders with enthusiasm.

Elizabeth didn't respond.

Lettie kicked her gently under the table. "Those of us who struggle to get on do what we must. Mr. Winders seems like a good man who will treat you well."

"Yes," Elizabeth said, "he's good to me, and I don't want anything to change. I made the mistake of telling Mr. Pimberton about it. He said I should take the position. Although he's shown no displeasure with our arrangement, I now know I've overstayed my welcome." She could kick *herself* for that.

"Tell Mr. Winders that Long Liz is no laced mutton," Lettie said. "Tell him that if you're to live with him, you don't want his money."

"Then I would have no freedom."

"You've had many interviews for positions in the last year, yet no one has offered you anything good enough. You can keep looking for another position and leave when you find one. I won't always work for Mrs. Huntermoon. As soon as I find a better situation, I'll leave her. The woman is quite mad, her and her demon, Eriot!"

Indeed, Elizabeth had had no luck finding another position that would provide the equivalent or reasonable alternative to the room and pay situation she had with Mr. Pimberton. At odd moments, she'd blamed her accent, and struggled to remove it from her speech. At other times, she decided that incidents of her ingratitude in the past had somehow left such a mark on her that others, even strangers, knew she was undeserving. But then that was ridiculous, since Lettie, Mr. Pimberton, and Mr. Winders had all been quite charitable in their treatment of her.

As Elizabeth sat in a state of gloom, Lettie went to the bar and ordered another glass of ale for each of them. Elizabeth had always limited herself to one glass of ale, even though she always wanted more. At present, however, she didn't have the strength to say no. By the time she had finished the second glass, she was in a much better mood.

"I don't know why I'm making such a fuss about Edward's offer."

"So, he's no longer Mr. Winders, eh?" Lettie said, laughing. "So you're thinking you'll take him up on it?"

"Yes," Elizabeth said. "Thank you for pouring some reason into me." She gestured toward the empty glass and giggled.

"You're welcome."

Elizabeth was intoxicated, yet not so much that she couldn't make her way home and ready herself to receive Mr. Winders that evening. Her earlier melancholy had come from the realization that she was so infatuated with Edward that she couldn't resist his invitation. She also feared that once she'd taken up with him, she would not be willing to leave for another position. But the ale had removed such trepidations, and that evening, over dinner at the Barley Mow, she formally agreed to his terms.

Terminating her employment with Mr. Pimberton, she removed to the constable's residence in Grafton Street, southeast of Marylebone Park, in early summer of 1867.

Mr. Edward Winders had two connecting ground floor rooms in a two story tenement. The place had been recently painted a light blue. The furnishings included a bed, an armoire and a small desk and chair in a bedroom with two curtained windows.

The other room had a table, three chairs, a small stove, cabinets with counters, one curtained window, and a door that let onto the street.

Mr. Winders introduced Elizabeth to his neighbors as his wife. When he did so, men frequently gave a knowing smile or smirk, while the women gave tight smiles or merely looked away.

"You mustn't worry yourself over their disapproval," Edward said. "If they were worth having as friends, they wouldn't judge harshly. They won't cause you any trouble because they want no trouble from me."

Elizabeth wasn't overly concerned—she'd seen such reactions many times in her days as a prostitute.

Clearly from the start, she understood that he meant for her to sleep with him, and worried that their sexual passions might become part of her domestic duties. Elizabeth promised herself that she would engage in sexual intercourse only when it pleased her. Not wanting to insult the man, however, she didn't bring up the subject with him.

You should be honest with your beau, Bess said. *Tell him about your past and he will know that you want to share everything with him, the good and the bad. It is the way of love.*

If you tell him about your past, he will hold it over you or turn you out, Liza said.

The honeymoon lasted for several months. Elizabeth pursued sex with Edward like a hunt. They bounded after climax as if it were a prey that must be run to ground, torn apart, and consumed. He gave as good as he got and they learned to synchronize their climaxes. They tried both sheep's gut and vulcanized rubber sheaths, but Elizabeth and Edward became so wild in their passion, the prophylactics frequently tore open, whatever the type.

Elizabeth was certain she would become pregnant. She was more concerned about the consequences of having to take care of a child than having one out of wedlock. On each occasion that Edward's seed spilled inside her, Elizabeth promised herself that the next time she would go easier, yet when that time came, the passion of the moment took over as it had before.

Edward wasn't particularly concerned. "I know what to do if you get knapped," he said. "I'll take care of you, don't you worry."

If you become pregnant, Bess said, *he'll marry you.*

He means, Liza said, *that he knows a butcher who can end a pregnancy.*

One evening as they lay in bed after an exhausting hour of sex, Elizabeth was feeling especially warm toward Edward. She decided to take Bess's advice, and told him all about her time as a prostitute. His reaction was far from expected. He was neither alarmed by the news nor pleased with her honesty.

"I knew something like that was hiding in your past," he said with little emotion. "You carry it in your eyes. I've seen enough bunters to recognize it. As long as you're healthy now, I'm not concerned."

Elizabeth was disappointed, although not sure why. Her worst fear—that he'd turn her out—wasn't realized. She'd told the truth despite the risk, but there was nothing in his response to indicate that he recognized that she'd given him a gift by trusting him with her past. She might as well have kept her mouth shut.

PC Winders worked a 10PM to 10AM shift. Each evening, he dressed in his dark blue uniform, gathered up his wooden truncheon, handcuffs, rattle, and his sooty bull's eye lantern, and left his rooms in Grafton Street to walk to his beat near the railway station construction site which had taken on the name of the parish in which it stood, St. Pancras.

Elizabeth slept when he was gone so she'd be awake when he got home. She prepared meals for him to be eaten in the morning and in the early evening before he left for work. In the afternoons while he slept, she cleaned and went to market. On most Saturdays, she had a luncheon at a tavern with Lettie.

One Saturday afternoon, after having three glasses of ale and feeling quite tipsy, Elizabeth stumbled back to the rooms in Grafton Street and fell asleep in a chair, her head resting on the table.

"Wake up, Elizabeth," Edward said, rousing her from slumber.

Her cheek and forehead were sore from resting on the hard oak.

He smelled her breath. "You've been drinking."

Elizabeth sat up straight and rubbed her eyes. She saw through the windows that night had fallen. She reached for a lie and Liza had one available. "I ate at the Barley Mow with Lettie. The corn pottage I ate tasted old. It must have been fermented, and with the glass of ale I had, it was too much."

Mr. Winders looked at her skeptically, and shook his head. "This Lettie is a ghost. You speak of her often, yet I've never met her. If she exists at all, she's a bad influence on you."

"I've had ale with *you* before."

"Yes, but not at midday, when you have duties. What shall I have for supper?"

Elizabeth realized she had nothing for him. "I'm sorry," she said. "I wasn't aware the hour was so late."

"It seems you're often unaware."

His disapproval, much like that of her father, suggested he had more to complain about than he was willing to express openly. Although she thought that cowardly, she didn't want him to list all of his grievances with her.

"Will you find something to eat on your way? There's the funny little man with the red cap in Euston Road. He's always there late with his cart, hawking meat puddings."

"Yes," Mr. Winders said with a stern look, "that would be good, though it will have to come out of your wages."

Elizabeth was surprised—she'd never seen such a hard side to the man.

"Don't frown," he said. "You've brought it on yourself."

He treats you like a child, Liza said, *as if he's never made a mistake.*

Yes, but he's right to be cross, Elizabeth thought.

He didn't speak to her again until he said goodbye as he left for work.

Elizabeth met her twin at the Barley Mow the following Saturday. Lettie didn't look happy, and she'd already begun to drink.

Elizabeth sat next to her and leaned on the table. "What's troubling you? Has Mrs. Huntermoon's demon got to you?"

"I've had word that William died in America." Fresh tears fell down her cheeks.

Elizabeth regretted her attempt at humor.

"I loved that man," Lettie said, "and he loved me. I knew that when he came home, he'd help me find the children, and we'd all be together again. Now that will never happen."

Elizabeth tried to put her arm around her. Lettie shrugged off the embrace.

"I hate them all," she said, "his blooming family, those bloody people he called friends, and my own sister for helping them take my children."

Elizabeth sat in silence until her twin's tears dried up.

"I'm sorry," Lettie said. "I know you're trying to comfort me. I've had my troubles since Wednesday and I'm tired of them. I intend to drink, and I'd like you to join me. What will you have?"

"I'll have ale," Elizabeth said. She knew the drink's strength.

Lettie got up, walked to the bar and fetched a glass of the brew.

On the previous Saturday, the edge of oblivion to which Elizabeth's three glasses of ale had transported her was quite pleasant. The consequences were not.

"I can only have two glasses," Elizabeth said. "Edward didn't like what he saw last week when I had three. I hadn't fixed his supper."

"What did he say?"

Elizabeth smiled. "That *you* are a bad influence. He had to eat at a kerbside cart. Took it out of my wages."

Lettie laughed. "Yes, I suppose I am a bad influence, but what of it? With people like him and my husband's family running our lives, we need a bit of rebellion."

"I thought you liked Edward."

"You know I've never met him. I only know what you've told me. Don't let him push you around. He must need you as much as you need him or it won't work. Don't you forget that."

Lettie was becoming drunk and loud. "You'll have a third glass today just to spite him."

Elizabeth shook her head almost imperceptibly, trying to say no to her own desire for more. She had firmly determined that two glasses of the beverage was her limit. Even so, as she finished her second glass, she had a sense that much-needed rest and an escape from the stresses of daily life were one more swallow away. As Lettie's mood lightened, and she told bawdy jokes and laughed, her manner called for Elizabeth to become boisterous with her. Elizabeth wanted to join her friend. Reticence held her back. She was concerned with what the other patrons would think of her if she let go the way Lettie was doing, even though no one was paying any attention to her friend. The singing at some of the tables was louder than Lettie's voice, and some patrons were certainly more uproarious.

Alcohol not only helped Elizabeth set aside her troubles, if she drank just enough, it also provided her with an exuberance that allowed her to express herself more openly, to laugh, and to love. She wanted to experience that again, and as Lettie poked and tickled her, Elizabeth's craving for alcohol increased.

"If you don't order another drink they'll put us out," Lettie said.

"We haven't eaten anything yet."

Lettie shrugged her shoulders.

Finally, Elizabeth gave in. She walked to the bar and ordered another glass of ale. Laughing and joking with her friend, she drank it within a short time.

Later, upon returning from the privy, another glass of the brew stood at her place on the table. Lettie wore an exaggerated look of innocence.

Elizabeth was excited to see the fresh full glass. She could easily imagine having so much alcohol that she might never awaken, and the thought was disturbing. With Lettie to see her through it, however, she wasn't afraid.

My friend will not let me come to harm, she decided. Elizabeth quaffed half of her glass at once.

Lettie walked Elizabeth home from their luncheon and left her at her doorstep in Grafton Street. Elizabeth let herself in, and with some difficulty remained conscious as she set about to prepare a supper for the constable. He usually awoke about eight o'clock in the evening, and she hoped to recover her wits by then. She struggled to do her work quietly, but was so clumsy that she dropped a plate on the table and then later a pot full of water and chopped potatoes that she was carrying to the stove. She was cleaning up the mess when he came out of the bedroom.

"You woke me early!" he said.

Elizabeth glanced up, unease rising in her throat and pinching her face. Mr. Winders came close, a curiosity in his eyes, and inhaled deeply through his nose. His mouth hardened, his eyes narrowed and his brow hung ominously above them for a moment as he looked at her silently.

Elizabeth wanted to get up and run from the tenement, yet she stayed put, on her knees, her fingers frozen in the process of reaching for a stray bit of potato.

"I should turn you out now," the constable said coldly.

"No," Elizabeth said as she got up and sat at the table, "I promise I won't drink again in the day."

"Not day or night," he said, his eyes pinning her to her chair. "As long as you're in my service, I forbid you to drink."

Unwilling to think about not drinking again, or being turned out into the street, Elizabeth simply nodded her head so he'd leave her alone.

She got her wish: He dressed, picked up his equipment and left early.

Elizabeth climbed in their bed and slept.

Mr. Winders was the constable at home ever after. He smelled Elizabeth's breath every evening when he got up from bed. Elizabeth gave up drinking again. Still, if she stumbled or mispronounced a word he looked at her suspiciously. Slowly but surely, along with their treatment of each other, their sexual relations turned off cold. Elizabeth felt lucky that she had not become pregnant.

Bess had been wrong in her assessment of Mr. Winders, and Liza had been right.

Elizabeth became more wary of Bess's advice.

19

IN HER PATH

In the autumn of 1868 Elizabeth had had enough of PC Winders and was looking for another position. She'd become so disgusted with the man that she had a perverse desire to get drunk again to force an end to the situation, but was afraid of finding herself on the street.

Lettie hadn't liked what she'd heard of the constable's behavior. She was doing her best to help Elizabeth find a new position.

"I want to introduce you to someone," Lettie said while they shopped at market together. "He's a handsome fellow named Jon Stride, a carpenter hired to repair the stairway and banister in Mrs. Huntermoon's house. He's looking for a wife."

Elizabeth turned away so her friend wouldn't see her frown. Mr. Winders made her so unhappy, she wasn't looking forward to taking up with another man.

"He asked if I was interested!" Lettie said, "He's not my kind of fellow—too soft spoken. I thought you might like to meet a man who isn't puffed up on himself. What do you say, Long Liz?"

Elizabeth shook her head.

"Meet him," Lettie said, "then decide."

With some persuasion, Elizabeth agreed. She met with Lettie and Jon Stride at Hyde Park, midday on a Tuesday in November. Following introductions, as small talk began, Elizabeth's bonnet was lifted by the wind and thrown onto the green off the path. Mr. Stride hurried after it. When he returned and gave the bonnet to Elizabeth, Lettie excused herself, saying she'd forgotten to run an errand for Mrs. Huntermoon. Elizabeth knew her friend had planned the exit.

Once Lettie had gone, Mr. Stride said, "Miss Gustavsson, Mrs. Watts said she told you I was looking for a wife. Please don't allow that to make you uneasy. If we get along, then perhaps we'll see each other again, and that's all there is to be expected, I should think."

Elizabeth had been a bit uncomfortable, wondering if he was sizing her up. His gaze was light and respectful. If he hadn't brought up the subject, she might have forgotten about it with time. "I'm not uneasy," she said.

He was close to six feet tall, with a thin, strong frame, fair skin, brown eyes, and hair almost black where it wasn't graying at the sides. With a strong brow and square chin, he was handsome.

They walked the paths of the park and talked. The conversation was pleasant enough, but Elizabeth had no real hope that he'd find her interesting. He asked her about herself and she gave out her history briefly, leaving out those things of which she was ashamed, and her current situation with Mr. Winders.

"I come from Sheerness, Kent," he told her, then paused when she raised her brows in a questioning look. "It's a town on the Isle of Sheppey. How did you travel when you came to London from Sweden?"

"A steamship that crossed the North Sea and passed up the Thames."

"Sheerness lies just south of where you entered the Thames."

The information meant little to her. Even so, she nodded out of politeness.

"I came to London to work on a property in Poplar that belongs to my father. The structure needs a lot of help, and though he is a splendid carpenter and shipwright—taught me everything I know—he can't do that kind of work anymore. He says the property is mine if I can make it whole again. I hope to open a shop to serve food and drink. Poplar is growing with more rail lines going in and the docks and warehouses receiving goods from the East."

Elizabeth decided he was a thoughtful fellow, willing to take a risk. Although somewhat reserved in manner, he was engaged in an adventure, having come from a faraway town to the bustling city of London to make a go of a little shop.

"Will you make a public house or tavern?"

"Oh, no," he said, shaking his head. "It's too small for all that. I was thinking of a pastry shop. Nothing too tender; shortbread, biscuits, scones, gingerbread, and fruitcake."

"Anything to drink?"

"Coffee, I should think."

Elizabeth stopped walking and took another look at Mr. Stride.

He stopped and turned. "Don't you like coffee?" he asked.

Elizabeth tried to remember if she'd ever told Lettie about her dream of opening a coffee shop.

Your friend has surely put him up to this, Liza said. *Mr. Stride is teasing you.*

But no, Elizabeth was certain she'd never mentioned it.

He has been placed in your path for a reason, Bess said.

"Yes, I do like coffee. I must say, I make the best coffee of anyone I've known."

"You'll have to make me a cup sometime."

Elizabeth thought for a moment about how to do that. "Are

you working on the stairway in Mrs. Huntermoon's house this afternoon?"

He nodded.

"And do I understand that she is away from home during the repairs."

"She's been gone for the week."

"I know a shop nearby where I can get coffee beans. Then, if you'd like, I'll walk you back to the house and we'll ask Lettie if I can have the kitchen long enough to make us all a cup."

"That would be delightful," he said with a big smile.

Realizing that she liked the man, Elizabeth smiled too.

Mr. Stride enjoyed his cup of coffee. He and Elizabeth got to know each other over the next few weeks during several meals at taverns in the afternoon and at pubs after eight o'clock in the evening. They continued to see one another through the winter. He listened to what she had to say and asked about her days and nights in a manner that told her he was interested in her wellbeing. She didn't offer much about the time she spent away from him, but he didn't pry. She'd told him she was a domestic servant for a family in Grafton Street, and that her agreement with her master was that she wouldn't see any gentlemen while in his employ. Elizabeth made sure her rendezvous with Mr. Stride occurred well away from her doorstep.

Either Mr. Stride didn't move on his women as fast as her previous beau had done or he was not romantically interested in her. He kept asking to see her, however, and discussing the plans for his enterprise.

"I would very much enjoy working in your shop one day," she told him more than once.

Mr. Stride merely smiled each time, and Liza counseled her

not to get her hopes up.

On February 1, 1869, he took her to see the property he was restoring. They'd crossed London west to east, about seven miles, in a growler. The hackney carriage wasn't as nice as the hansom cab Mr. Winders preferred, being louder and less open. Still, Elizabeth and Mr. Stride traveled in reasonable comfort for the hour and a half it took for them to arrive at their destination.

The structure, a tiny two-room building with a shop front, was situated between two tenements in Chrisp Street, Poplar, the East End of London. The interior was stuffy. The front room was empty except for small drifts of sawdust. The chamber in the rear had no window. Mr. Stride lit a lamp so she could see it. Lumber, sawhorses, a miter box, various other tools and hardware were organized neatly within. A door in the far wall no doubt let onto a yard or alley. A fireplace occupied the south wall. The place didn't look like much, yet Elizabeth could imagine what it would be like when the work was finished, the food and drinks, the customers, and the money changing hands.

"I will easily sell food and drink through the front window," Mr. Stride said proudly. "Poplar has plenty of activity, workers coming and going from the docks, the rail yard, and the workhouse."

"People don't want to stand on the street to eat and drink," Elizabeth said.

He raised his brows as if he felt challenged, but then he pursed his lips and tilted his head as if waiting to hear more.

"They prefer to sit. You should open up the front room and put in a couple of tables. Put a window in between the two rooms and serve your drinks and pastries from the rear."

He looked into the distance, and his clean-shaved chin jutted forward as he seemed to consider her suggestions. "Not only do you make a fine cup, you have good ideas for serving. Let's look at other coffee shops to see what they're like."

Over the next week, they visited eight coffee shops and

discussed further ideas.

"This coffee isn't very good," Elizabeth said as they sat in a shop in a small lane between Oxford and Broad Streets.

She watched Mr. Stride looking around the establishment, politely watching the women and sizing up the men. Something about his manner allowed his unabashed gaze to appear unthreatening. He looked squarely at those of a higher class without the slightest risk of rebuke. She liked his confidence, and got the sense that he thought he was as good as anyone else. Elizabeth wished she felt the same way about herself.

"This drink is bitter," she said. "If coffee sits too long after it's been prepared for drinking, the color of the liquid turns a little gray. Do you see, it's not the warm brown it should be?"

Mr. Stride, still looking around, nodded his head with a slight smile.

"If I were serving, I'd have thrown this out and made fresh coffee for my patrons."

His smile grew to a grin.

"Am I funny?" she asked.

"No, but you've got the job if you want it. You plainly do."

Elizabeth pretended ignorance, and Mr. Stride sat back and looked at her squarely.

"I've depended solely on my own counsel for many years now and not always for the best," he said. "The desire for something different has come on me only recently. What do you think about you and me making that coffee shop of yours, and starting a family together? Would you marry me?"

He was so matter-of fact that she didn't believe him at first. Then the warmth of his smile persuaded her that he truly did want her. Her throat became clogged with all the words she might say and nothing came out.

"I suspect you've had troubles in your past," he continued, "as have I. I don't expect to know everything about you, although I hope we can be honest with each other. I know I enjoy your company very much, and that waking up to your sweet face will brighten my days."

She blinked rapidly to prevent tears from spilling.

At forty-eight years of age, Mr. Stride was twenty-three years her senior, and, no doubt, set in his ways, but he was a gentle man who looked upon her with respect. He had a bearing next to which she was proud to stand. He expected to have children, and while she had trepidations about her worthiness as a mother, she would not let that get in her way. The idea of having children with the man gave her hope for the future. With Mr. Stride by her side, she would become a different, more capable, and loving person.

You'd better keep your secrets well, Liza said, *or he won't be so proud to stand with you.*

If you are honest with him, he'll love you all the more, Bess said. *Don't hide your past from him.*

Elizabeth was inclined to believe that Liza was the more astute when it came to men. She was paying little attention to her voices at present, however, as she struggled to prevent herself from shouting her delight.

Finally, she composed herself and said simply, "Yes."

He reached across the table and grasped her hands. "You've made me very happy."

As jubilant as she was, Elizabeth knew that her relationship with Mr. Stride had already begun in falsehood. Her betrothed would probably be more concerned about the competition Mr. Winders represented than the fact that she was living with the man out of wedlock. Still, she felt compelled to bury the truth.

That evening, after Mr. Winders had gone to work, Elizabeth walked the few miles to Mr. Pimberton's house in Ledbury Road and sat on his step as she'd done three years earlier, waiting for him to return home from work.

When he arrived, he seemed happy to see her. He made a show of looking at his watch, then he looked back at her with a smile. "Miss Gustavsson, I recently played in the orchestra for a drama about a man traveling backward in time. For a moment, I thought I was that man."

"No, sir," she said. "but I've come to ask you to take me back temporarily."

He looked confused.

"My situation with Mr. Winders has gone badly. I won't go into it because I know you are—"

"He's caused trouble for more than one woman I know."

Why didn't he tell you about that before, Liza asked. *Men only look out for each other.*

"You wouldn't have to pay me, and I'd still do the charring. I'll marry in early March and would leave you then."

"Congratulations, Miss Gustavsson." He nodded his head and clasped his hands. "I'm happy to have you next door, and will gladly pay you as before."

"Thank you, sir," Elizabeth said. She had a lot to look forward to, although she had difficulty seeing beyond the conflict that lay just ahead.

The evening of the next day, Elizabeth spoke to Mr. Winders as she served his supper. "Mr. Pimberton would have me back."

He was silent for some time, then he turned and looked at her. She was prepared for a bad reaction, even the possibility of a fight, yet he merely shrugged. "We haven't got along for some time," he said.

There's evidence of how much he cared for you, Liza said. *Men are capricious. Be careful with your new one. Only tell him what you must.*

Before Mr. Winders left for work, he turned to her again. She thought he would give some parting words, but instead, his right fist shot forward and struck her in the jaw. His angry face rose above her as she fell back. Elizabeth balled up on the floor to defend against further harm, covering her head with her arms. She heard the door open and close, and after waiting another moment in silence, she looked up. Mr. Winders had gone. She had a tooth loose in the left side of her lower jaw.

Elizabeth packed her belongings. What she couldn't carry with her, she left behind and would never see again.

As she walked to Mr. Pimberton's house, looking forward to her March 7th wedding date with Mr. Stride helped distract her from the pain in her jaw. She was headed for something better, something *much* better.

20

A SHOP OF HER OWN

Elizabeth and Jon were wed in a small ceremony at St. Giles in the Fields Church, with two witnesses provided by the presiding reverend. Afterward, she lived with Jon for a short time at a tenement in Hampstead Road. They set out with a vigor to conceive children. He was not as experienced as Mr. Winders, yet with help from Elizabeth, Jon slowly developed into a serviceable lover.

She had hardly settled into her new home when word came that a room had become free in the tenement just north of Mr. Stride's shop. He'd appealed to the landlords of the tenements on either side of his property for a room almost a year earlier. His planning and patience had paid off at the right time.

Over the course of a week, Elizabeth and Jon removed to the new second floor room in the tenement beside the shop in May of 1869. The place wasn't much. A single window looked out onto laundry lines that crisscrossed the space at the rear of the block of buildings above a courtyard that held a dozen or more lavatory sheds. The building formed a "U" shape around the courtyard, with a gap that led to the street. The small coal grate fireplace in one wall of the room didn't draw well. When the wind was strong outdoors, entering the courtyard through the gap and rattling the windows, Elizabeth and Jon had a choice of enduring the smoke that accumulated in the room or opening the window and suffering a reek lifted from the privy sheds below. The room was drafty, and the walls and floors were so thin they could understand what their neighbors said even at conversational volumes.

Elizabeth found a public bath house within a quarter mile of the new room, a much easier walk than the nearly one half mile to the one nearest the old room. Jon went to the public baths once a week without having to be reminded, unlike Mr. Winders who would have gone several weeks if Elizabeth had not browbeaten him into bathing more regularly.

Jon left home most days to work as a carpenter in various locations. In his spare time, he worked on the shop and Elizabeth helped. At night, after supper, they continued their quest for children.

One evening as Jon was having difficulty reaching climax, Elizabeth inserted a finger into his rectum and quickly brought him to release. When he'd recovered from the thrill, he looked at her suspiciously.

"That was truly a wonderful feeling," he said, "but how did you know…" His voice trailed off as he seemed unable to form the question fully.

Elizabeth knew her features betrayed her distress with the question. Liza was taking her time. Finally, the voice came forth with something for her to say. "I've not told you this because I didn't want you to think poorly of me or my family," Elizabeth said. She thought her expression of distress worked well with what she would say. "My mother was a prostitute before she married my father. She taught me a few things."

Jon swallowed, frowned, and sat up. He was quiet for a moment, then said, "That doesn't seem like the sort of thing a mother would teach her daughter."

Elizabeth shrugged and moved quickly to clean herself at the basin. Sensing his unease and knowing he wanted to ask more questions, she kept her face turned away. Eventually, the tension left the room.

Elizabeth had not seen her twin in over a month. Lettie came to see Elizabeth at her new home in the tenement in Chrisp Street and was shown the work in progress on the shop.

"Jon and I have found suppliers for the pastries and coffee we want to serve," Elizabeth said as Lettie looked around. "We bought the cutlery and dishes we'll need for serving our—" She put her left hand to her jaw to soothe a sudden pain.

Lettie must have seen her grimace. "Is the tooth still troubling you?"

"Yes, I should have it out, though I'm afraid I'll lose more if I do."

Elizabeth led Lettie into the room in the rear and showed her a new coffee grinder with a big hopper and a large coffee roasting cylinder that turned with a hand crank. The grinder was bolted to a table in a corner with a bowl of ground beans under it. The roaster, already blackened from use in the fireplace, sat on the hearth.

"Jon had to make improvements to the flue to make room for the contraption. I've spent many hours grinding beans and perfecting my roast. The devices are top notch. I didn't ask about the expense, but Jon weighs each purchase carefully. I believe he's investing the bulk, if not all, of his savings."

"You've found a good man, Long Liz, one willing to risk

everything for you," Lettie said.

She's right, Bess said, *you must risk everything for him as well.*

Not if you want to keep him, Liza said.

"Yes, he's a good man," Elizabeth said. "I'm not certain I deserve him. There are things..." She stopped and shook her head, still unwilling to talk about her deepest shame.

Lettie allowed silence, then said, "Something is bothering you; something besides that tooth that needs out. You'll tell me one day, I know you will. Whatever it is, I won't think the less of you for knowing it."

Elizabeth pressed her lips together tightly.

"Speaking of good men," Lettie said, "I have a new beau, Mr. Joseph Snelling. He's in the Royal Navy. Let's hope he's as good a man as the one you found."

"I do hope so," Elizabeth said. "I met Jon thanks to you, and I've never been so grateful."

Lettie waved away Elizabeth's words, patted her belly, and said, "I need a tightener. Let's find a new tavern for our luncheons."

"What shall we call our enterprise?" Jon asked, as the repairs to the building and preparations for the shop neared completion.

"I've been thinking about that," Elizabeth said. "I once worked for a gentleman named Olovsson. I was the maid of all work for his family in Gothenburg. Herr Olovsson liked my coffee. He told me that one day I should have my own shop. Later, he helped me when I was destitute, finding a position for me—the one I held just before coming to England."

"Olovsson," Jon said, as if trying out the name.

"Yes," Elizabeth said. "Olovsson's Coffee Shop sounds good to me."

Jon was silent for a moment, then said, "If he meant that

much to you, then, yes, that would be a fine name."

He prepared a framed wooden surface, carefully painted the name of their new shop on it in bright blue, then hung it on the front of the small building.

Elizabeth wrote to Fru Leena Jensson and told her about her new life. She included in her post an envelope containing a message for Herr Olovsson—one that told about the coffee shop and the name she'd given it. She requested that Fru Jensson pass the envelope on to the gentleman. She hoped he would be proud of her, and happy to have his name on the establishment.

The shop in Chrisp Street opened in June of 1869. The quality of Elizabeth's coffee drink was higher than that of other coffee houses in the area. Before long Olovsson's Coffee Shop had a regular clientele. For the next year, as problems cropped up, Elizabeth and Jon worked well together to solve and learn from the difficulties. They went through several pastry suppliers before finding one that provided goods of consistent quality. The caliber of coffee they got, even from the best supplier, varied some, but Elizabeth sorted the beans and blended them for the best results. She stayed well away from alcoholic drink, even when Jon partook and encouraged her to join him. They worked hard and their efforts paid off; the business was growing and they were soon enjoying an increasing income. Jon gave up carpentry and devoted his days to helping run the coffee shop. Elizabeth had found the something better she'd been looking for and, for the nonce, she was happy.

21

DAYS, MONTHS, YEARS OF HARD WORK

Elizabeth's damaged tooth became so loose, she had to have it out. Jon helped her remove it by the string and doorknob method.

The angry constable left his mark on you, Liza said. *Every time you notice the gap between your teeth, you'll think of him. If he knew, he'd be pleased.*

Elizabeth would have liked to blame Bess for the loss—for having encouraged her to live with Mr. Winders—yet she'd only be blaming herself.

Elizabeth never heard back from Fru Jensson or Herr Olovsson. She wondered if they had received her correspondence.

In mid-1870, the price of coffee beans was on the rise. Jon had heard from suppliers that a fungus, known as rust, was decimating the coffee crops in Ceylon, from which the bulk of

British trade in the beans came. Olovsson's Coffee Shop tried to charge more per cup to compensate for the loss, but they began to lose customers, and were forced to drop the price back to what it had been.

By the autumn, Jon was taking carpentry jobs again, sometimes being gone for days on end when sleeping near job sites that were too far away from home. The labor in the shop was almost more than Elizabeth could handle when he was away. Despite the hardships, she kept the place going.

Lettie and her new gentleman, Mr. Joseph Snelling, were wed. Elizabeth was in attendance. Jon was away, staying near a distant job site. Once the couple was married, Elizabeth saw less of Lettie for a time.

Toward the end of 1870, Jon was wondering why Elizabeth had not become pregnant.

"Do you have any reason to think you should be having trouble?" he asked. They were cleaning up after closing the shop for the evening on a day in November.

Elizabeth thought again about the stillbirth at Kurhuset and her venereal disease. Syphilis by itself should not have rendered her infertile. If she'd had other venereal diseases simultaneously, there was the possibility that she had indeed lost the ability to bear children. She certainly was exposed to a great many risks during that time period.

Accuse him, Liza suggested, as Elizabeth stacked dishes and sorted utensils.

"I've heard that a man with a crook in his member will not sire easily," she said in an exasperated tone. "Don't blame me for *your* problems."

When she was finished speaking, Jon's silence unnerved her more than his stare. Finally he said, "I've never heard such a thing before. For all you know on the subject of getting jiggy, you must have spent your young life in study." He shook his head and turned away, then grumbled, "Besides, it's not that crooked."

Elizabeth felt bad about making him doubt himself.

She had rarely spoken of her history for fear that unsavory aspects of her young life might get out. On several occasions, though, she'd revealed some bit of knowledge that most decent women should not possess. Jon had the good manners not to pry, but she could tell that the increasing number of revelations had left him mistrustful. He wasn't a prude. Although at times she had wanted to take Bess's advice and be honest with him about the past, Elizabeth wasn't ready to risk her husband's disapproval.

In her desire to end the discussion, she threw utensils into the water in the washtub. She banged dishes together.

"I'm sorry," Jon said, gently putting his hands on her waist. "It doesn't do any good to cast blame."

Elizabeth was slow to put away her frustration, yet she turned to Jon and allowed him to embrace her.

In January 1871, Jon was called home to Sheerness by his father to help repair a ship for the Royal Navy, HMS Megaera. He would be gone for several weeks.

"I don't think I can hold the shop together for that long by myself," Elizabeth said.

They lay together on the straw mattress of their bed after a long hard day. His carpentry job was close enough that he'd made it home by midnight. He still had sawdust in his hair, and the particles made the bed uncomfortable. Elizabeth didn't complain. She was glad he was home for the night. Jon held her and slid his left leg between her legs all the way to her crotch. The warmth of his body against hers on such a chilly night was a pleasure to be savored.

"I must go," he said. "The pay is greater than what I earn in the city. We need it to keep the shop going. If the price for coffee gets much higher, we'll be paying customers to drink it. Your coffee is what brings them in. We won't do well just serving tea."

Elizabeth began to protest again, but he put his mouth on hers. Within moments he had entered her, and she had nothing further to say.

Lettie came to the coffee shop to visit on a Sunday in February. Jon had not yet returned from Sheerness. Elizabeth was cleaning up and making preparations to open the shop the next morning. She had roasted the coffee she'd need for the next week, and was grinding the beans. When Elizabeth's arm became sore turning the crank handle, her twin took over for her.

"I'm knapped," Lettie said with a guilty expression—she knew about the difficulties Elizabeth was having with Jon about getting pregnant.

Without pause in her cranking, Elizabeth said without reservation, "Congratulations!"

"It couldn't come at a worse time." Lettie spoke as if a little bad news might prevent envy. "Joseph is leaving on a voyage to Australia."

"That's wretched luck." Thinking of her arguments with Jon, however, Elizabeth wished briefly that she were so unlucky, and that gave her a humorous idea. "You could stand in for me for a while. We look so much alike, Jon will never know, and he'll be so pleased to think his wife is expecting."

"You are a funny woman, Long Liz." Lettie chuckled, then was silent for a time, her thoughts far away and her expression shifting as though she were puzzling something out.

Her arm sore, Elizabeth stepped away from the grinder.

Lettie seemed to emerge from her reverie to take over at the crank handle. "Joseph is in Sheerness now," she said. "I wonder if he will run into Jon. They've never met, so they won't know each other even if they do."

"When does he leave for Australia?"

"I don't know. He'd already left, but his ship was damaged in a storm and put in for repairs."

"His ship is under repair in Sheerness?"

"Yes, HMS Megaera, I think."

"That's the ship Jon's working on."

"Good—I feel much better about it."

Elizabeth nodded and smiled. "Curious."

When Jon returned from Sheerness in late February, he had a possible plan for their future. "We might sell the property and move the shop closer to the docks. I spoke to a gentleman named Pelham in Sheerness who owns a property closer to the London docks in High Street. That's closer to all those laborers who need your coffee to help them wake up in the morning." He had a big smile like a hawker trying to sell something that had gone bad.

"Pelham's place needs work. It's bigger than ours, worth more, but he might be willing to make a trade so he doesn't have all the expense of repairs to his place. Sounds like we might operate the shop and live in the property if it works out. Father likes the plan, and will draw up the papers if we go through with it. I have a meeting with Pelham in a week."

Elizabeth nodded her head enthusiastically, and he seemed surprised.

"Even if it works out, it'll be a lot of work," Jon warned, a bit deflated since he didn't need to pitch so hard. His duffer's smile was gone and his enthusiasm for his plan had cooled slightly. Perhaps his doubts were surfacing. Elizabeth could see that he was tired from his travels and all the hard work. For the first time, she could see the years wearing on him.

"We already have a lot of hard work," she said, "There's no reason we can't do it in another place."

Jon and Mr. Pelham came to an agreement. Elizabeth continued to run the Chrisp Street coffee shop through the spring, while Jon made repairs to the storefront portion of the new property. In the evenings they moved their belongings from the Chrisp Street tenement to the large loft above the rear room of the new property. Although the loft would be their new home, it would be repaired last since they needed to get the shop opened quickly.

"With the warm weather coming, the holes in the walls won't be so bad," Jon told Elizabeth as he showed her around her future home. "The holes in the floors are dangerous, but I've discovered the extent of the rot, and, you see," he said, pointing, "I've marked the edges with white paint. The beams underneath are solid enough. The floorboards aren't, so don't walk there."

As bad as it looked, Elizabeth could see the hope in Jon's eyes, and was reassured.

By the beginning of summer, they were out of the old property and committed to the new. The coffee shop was slow for the first few weeks. Following that, they were doing better than at the old location. Jon had repaired the floor in the loft, yet still needed to replace the temporary patches in the walls with more permanent materials.

The teeth on either side of the one Elizabeth had lost after being struck by Mr. Winders became loose and began to ache in her lower left jaw. She was miserable until mid-July when she could stand the pain no longer, and begged Jon to pull the teeth. They weren't loose enough for the string and doorknob method. He fetched his pliers and a bottle of whiskey for her pain. Elizabeth refused the drink.

In August while Jon was away, Lettie came to the shop on a Sunday to help with coffee preparations. She was clearly troubled. "Joseph's ship," Lettie said, "the Megaera, has been wrecked on St. Paul's Island in the Pacific. The crew is stranded. There are too many for all to be rescued at once. They have supplies, but must survive until help comes."

"We'll hope for the best," Elizabeth said, embracing her friend.

"I'm sure he'll be fine," Lettie said, her eyes glistening as tears threatened.

Jon came home early on a Thursday in September. "I lost a job today because some-bloody-one told my client that I worked on the Megaera." He was spitting mad. "The story of the wreck is in the *Illustrated London News!* I tried to tell him the hull was what had failed and I didn't work on that part of the ship. He wouldn't have it. Let's hope he doesn't spread the word."

Whether Jon's client did or not, word got out, and it had a detrimental effect on his reputation as a carpenter right when they needed the income the most. The price of coffee had continued to climb. Olovsson's Coffee Shop tried again to raise what they charged for their products. The competition took business from them when they did, however. Again, they were forced to restore the old prices. Despite the increased numbers of patrons at the coffee shop, Elizabeth was working harder, selling more coffee, but earning less per cup. At least she had his help on the days when Jon had no other work.

The final repairs to the loft were made in October 1871. Their one room dwelling above the shop was homey if nothing else, with a corner hutch for clothing and linens, a chest for blankets and sundries, a large bed Jon had constructed of cherry wood, a table and chairs, a small desk, shelves, a curtained window, and a Persian rug. Elizabeth and Jon celebrated with a romp in bed. Afterward, while they lay side by side, enjoying the warmth of a room with no drafts, Jon said, "Perhaps if you saw a doctor, we might find out something we could do to help you become pregnant."

Elizabeth tried to laugh off the suggestion. "We already know how to make babies," she said. "You were good tonight."

"No, I mean there might be something wrong a doctor could fix."

Elizabeth feared that a doctor's examination might reveal something of her history, that the physician might see some evidence of her venereal disease and have a talk with Jon about it.

"I won't suffer a crow to examine my most private self," she said with a touch of outrage.

Jon's face became tight with anger. "I don't think you want very much to become a mother. Why do you think I work so hard if not to give what I build to my children?"

Elizabeth matched his anger with her own. "I would hope you do it for us, as well! I'm not merely breeding stock, am I?"

"Of course not, yet I made it clear to you that I wanted a family."

"Have I not met your every effort toward that end?"

"Well, yes, but your behavior—your words..."

"Words do not make children."

"No, but it's as if you're hiding something."

"Because I don't want to be looked upon as half a woman?" Elizabeth wanted him to believe she saw his questions as an insult to her womanhood, even though her anger was, in truth, at herself. She feared that as a consequence of her own actions as a young adult, she had thrown away the precious gift of motherhood. Looking again at the possibility, she had difficulty maintaining her self-righteousness, and Jon seemed to see that.

"Do you believe you cannot have children?"

"I *don't* know."

He turned away and went downstairs. When she heard sawing, she presumed that he was continuing his work on the damaged rear door frame.

Elizabeth blamed their irritability on the stresses of long hard hours and low income. Since the damage to Jon's reputation as a carpenter, he was forced to take work of lesser pay, doing smaller projects that required less skill. His pride had suffered, and Elizabeth felt sorry for him. She promised herself that she'd find a way to approach him with the truth about her past. Elizabeth also decided that the present wasn't the time to do so.

Lettie was not faring well either. She had her child in early November, a baby boy she named Martin. Then word came that Joseph Snelling had perished on St. Paul's Island, and the half pay she'd been receiving from the Royal Navy ceased.

On a Sunday evening in February of 1872, she was again in the back room of the coffee shop, helping Elizabeth make her weekly roast and grind. "I have had to go to my sister, Mary, every month for help since Martin was born," Lettie said. "She'll give me assistance, but she must first question me and tell me how to live my life before she hands it over. I hate her for helping William's family take my children from me. She can see how I feel about her and so she draws out the weekly interview to gain satisfaction. It's all I can do to keep from harming her. If I had a knife with me, I might slit her throat." She barked out an uneasy laugh.

Elizabeth was surprised. Lettie had always been a steady rock, an island surrounded by calm in the sea of struggle and change that was Elizabeth's life in London. With her twin and Jon so unhappy lately, she experienced the feeling that no safe harbor existed for her, something she hadn't felt in a long time.

Jon extracted two more teeth from Elizabeth's lower left jaw in the autumn of 1872.

Elizabeth was cleaning up the coffee shop after hours on September 7, 1873 when a boy appeared, knocking at the locked front door. She unlocked the door and gave the boy a farthing in exchange for a message on a piece of blue paper. The boy looked at the tiny coin, spat on the ground at Elizabeth's feet, and ran off into the night.

The message told of the death of Jon's father. She gave it to her husband when he returned late in the evening. After he'd read it, he settled into a chair at the table where they ate their meals. "Most of my dreams have been dashed," he said. "Much in life has not gone my way, though I had hoped that my father would see my children one day."

Sitting across from him at the table, Elizabeth was crushed by his words and the look of hurt in his eyes. They had not spoken of children in over a year, and her promise to herself to tell him about her past had been conveniently forgotten. She broke down weeping, and lowered her head to the tabletop.

Jon was silent for a long while, then he said, "It's not your fault."

Elizabeth tried to compose herself to speak. "But it is," she said, finally.

"No, no," he held her hand, and reached to lift her face.

When she could look him in the eye, she said, "I was gravely ill when I was younger. The ability to bear children must have been taken from me then."

"You knew?" He looked confused.

"Well, no."

"Yet you suspected?" He released her and his face strained toward a grimace.

"Yes," Elizabeth said quickly, then too loudly, "I'm sorry!"

He swallowed hard and sat back, a stiffness in his frame. "You've not told me how you became so ill."

She hesitated, covered her mouth with her hand, and said, "I am too afraid to tell you."

"We've never made a big show of it," he said at last, "but I thought you *loved* me."

"Of course, I do." Elizabeth became aware that she gripped the edge of the table tightly when her hand began to hurt from the effort.

"Then why didn't you trust me with your suspicion?"

She let go of the table and sat back. At present, she couldn't look at him. "Because I *do* love you, Jon. I know you'll want to know why I have that suspicion, and I'm afraid I'll lose you when you have the answer."

He looked down at his hands in his lap, and sat quietly for a long time. The longer his silence stretched on the more unsettling Elizabeth found it. Still, she could not will herself to get up and move away from him. Indeed, she hardly took a breath as she waited, because she knew that what he said at the end of that silence would determine her future.

Thankfully, the voices of her two selves also remained silent.

Sounds of movement in the street out front found their way to her. She heard a door slamming in a nearby building and a whistle from a train or a boat. The air had become colder, and the light dimmer.

The floor under Jon's chair creaked. He seemed to become interested in why, as a carpenter might. He rocked a bit in his chair and listened. Finally, he looked up and said quietly, "I should have told you about the mistakes I made when I was young, terrible things I did long before we met, how I frightened myself and my family. Then you would have felt more at ease telling about yourself."

He cleared his throat, and looked her in the eye. "Keep your secret if you need to."

Starved for air, Elizabeth took a deep breath. She clutched for him as he reached across the table and took her trembling hands.

"I do love you, Elizabeth," he said. "Your sweet face *has* brightened my days."

Tears of relief spilled down Elizabeth's cheeks. She moved quickly into the warmth and safety of his arms.

With the death of his father, some of the glint had gone from Jon's eyes. He suffered increasingly from sore joints, aching muscles, shortness of breath, and pains in the chest. Elizabeth blamed herself for his declining health. She worked harder and asked for his help less. The couple struggled with the coffee shop for another year and finally sold it.

22

HISTORIES

Elizabeth and Jon moved into a single room in a tenement in Giraud Street in January 1875. One night, shortly after they were situated in the room, Jon sat her down and told her a story from his youth.

"In my twenties, me and some pals were taken with the tales of the highwaymen and dragsmen at Blackheath. We formed a gang of footpads, and found a spot on the road to Margate to prey upon the coaches coming and going from London."

Jon looked at Elizabeth and shook his head vigorously. He lowered his head and shouted into his cupped hands, "Fools, we were!"

His lips were pressed together hard when he looked up again and Elizabeth was afraid he'd stop the tale. She leaned forward and took his hands for encouragement.

He turned away, and continued. "No one was to be harmed. We just wanted their valuables. We wore sacks on our faces, yet somehow my family found out about our adventures. My father threatened to turn me out in the street. I lied to him and kept at it."

Jon was gazing out their room's single window as if he could see in the street outside the events of his recollection. "One night we stopped a coach and out stepped a cocksure swell. My pal, Robert, our leader, held a pistol on the man, but he wouldn't hand over his wallet and watch. Instead, he pushed Robert." Jon grimaced and lowered his head again. "Robert looked worried. He kept waving his iron at the man and demanding his valuables, and the toff kept pushing him. Finally he pushed so hard, Robert fell on his arse." Jon was silent for a time, then he looked squarely at Elizabeth, a deep regret in his eyes. "The pistol went off and the gentleman died," he said in a rush. "We ran away and none of us was ever charged. I quit those fellows and took up carpentry with Father. No one ever knew what I'd done except for my pals and now you. I never suffered punishment for my crime. I've tried to do right since."

Jon covered his face with his hands. Elizabeth leaned her head against his shoulder. He took her in his arms briefly, then released her and left the room, heading out into the night. He didn't return until late, long after Elizabeth had gone to bed.

The next evening, she found a moment that seemed right to tell Jon about meeting Klaudio, her prostitution, her syphilis, and the stillbirth of her girl, Beata. She began six times, only to break off after the first few words to take deep breaths and think of a better way to start. Finally, she had the words and they poured out of her.

Jon didn't turn away, and as she paused before trying to speak of her darkest secret, the death of Fru Andersdotter, he said, "Thank you for trusting me."

Bess had been right when she'd suggested that Elizabeth risk everything by being honest with Jon, and Liza had been wrong.

The cynical voice knew nothing of love. She would never

have good advice about friendship or romance.

Elizabeth knew that Jon thought she was done. She wished she were, as the wave of shame that always accompanied the recollections of the old woman's death took hold of her. Drowning in the shameful memories—lighting fires in the stove and fireplace of Hortense's house to cover up her own absence, lying to Herr Rikhardsson about awakening to find the woman dead, being rewarded with a position of employment on that day for merely being associated with the woman—Elizabeth collapsed upon the bed and closed her eyes.

Jon caressed her cheek, her shoulder, and with time, she relaxed and let go of the memories. He thought she was done, and she would take advantage of that, despite her revelation that Bess's advice about honesty had been sound.

She was relieved that Jon took what truth she had offered so well. Although she felt at least partly unburdened, she was in despair over her inability to face the old woman's death.

Elizabeth felt differently toward Jon once she'd heard his tale. Despite his bent posture, a loss of muscle tone, and his frequent downcast looks, he was her hero as never before. He'd had his adventure early in life and learned from it. Although Jon was far from perfect, he had a big heart, and had made every effort to have a full life. She was proud to have him, and regretted only that she'd been unable to give him children.

They didn't have much over the next few years, yet were closer than they'd ever been. Jon took on what carpentry jobs he could find, but as his health declined, he was capable of less and less. Deciding that she would take on whatever work she could to lighten his load, working several jobs if necessary, gave her a strong sense of purpose.

Elizabeth worked for a time for John Hale, the man who bought Olovsson's Coffee Shop. He'd kept the name. She roasted and ground beans for him. When the establishment was busy, she helped serve customers. Hale allowed her to advertise to his customers that she offered sewing services. She mended clothing in the evenings and did simple alterations. When Olovsson's Coffee Shop finally failed, she took short term work of all sorts, sewing, charring, and scouring, while trying to find employment serving within a household. She could not interview for most positions, however, because she was married.

Lettie's fortunes were far worse. Mrs. Huntermoon passed away and, consequently, Lettie lost her position. She fell to working as a scourer at a laundry while she looked for employment within another household. Her child, Martin, died of a fever before he was three years old.

Neither of the two Elizabeths had any luck finding a position. What short term work they found, they often shared.

Lettie sat in Elizabeth's room one evening in the summer of 1876 helping to mend clothes. Jon had not yet returned from a job erecting a sign over a new sweet shop.

"After I lost my position with Mrs. Huntermoon, I was so poor, I became afraid for Martin. I thought I might not be able to provide for him. One day I did a foolish thing; I left him on my sister, Mary's, doorstep in a basket. I thought she'd take care of him better than I could."

Elizabeth was shocked, and she allowed it to show on her face. She opened her mouth to say that she and Jon would have helped. Lettie spoke first.

"I didn't abandon him," she said. "I knocked on her door and hid around the corner of the building, watching. Mary came to the door. She saw my boy in the basket, then turned around, left him, and went back inside. I thought she'd come back, but she didn't, so I gathered him up and took him home."

"Perhaps you should have spoken to her about taking care of Martin first."

"No." Lettie shook her head. "I can't talk to my sister. She helped William's family take my children because she thought I wouldn't be a good mother. Mary has always thought of me as foolish. Nothing I do is done well enough, except for one thing. I did something for which she cannot forgive me."

"What's that?" Elizabeth asked.

Lettie waved the question away. "She should have at least taken Martin in from the cold. I'd brought him to see her twice before, so she couldn't pretend she didn't know who he was."

"You should have come to us for help."

"Like me, you and Jon have precious little. My sister's a scurf."

Elizabeth gave Lettie a questioning look.

"She's cruel to those she employs." She shook her head as if frustrated. "She does help me—two shillings a week—but if I have to keep seeing her to get it, I will surely kill her."

"You don't mean that," Elizabeth said.

"Don't I?" Lettie took a deep breath. She glanced at Elizabeth curiously.

Elizabeth became uncomfortable as her friend's gaze lingered. "Stop it," she said.

"I'm sorry," Lettie said, "I'm getting a good look at you for a reason. I have an idea you're not going to like. Still, It's bene bone."

"So mysterious!"

"Wait and see. I've thought about it for a long time."

"Tell me." Elizabeth was impatient.

"I visit my sister once a week now. She's lonely and bitter, she's vindictive, yet she's honor-bound to help me. I know she couldn't live with herself if she thought I was suffering anything other than what I suffer at her own hands. This is because she believes I saved her life at risk of my own when we were little. That is the one thing I did right, and she'll never forgive me for it or perhaps it's that she can't forgive herself for needing my help."

"Please, tell me what happened," Elizabeth said.

Lettie paused and took a deep breath. "When we were young, we were playing on a steep hill when she fell. She rolled down toward a small spring and I ran after her. A black adder came from the rocks around the spring and bit her on the hand. I stepped on the snake and tried to kick it away, but it bit me on the leg. Mary became insensible from the poison. I crushed the snake's head and carried Mary home. When she mistreats me, I sometimes prey upon her sympathies with that story." Lettie displayed an evil grin.

"What does all that have to do with me?"

Lettie hesitated for a moment. "I want you to go in my stead and I'll give you half of what she gives me."

Elizabeth shook her head. "Why should she give the money to me?"

"Well, I know you won't like this." Lettie took another deep breath. She had a peculiar smile. "I want you to pretend you're me when you go see her."

"That's absurd," Elizabeth said with an uneasy laugh. "She'll know I'm not you."

"She's nearsighted. Don't get too close."

"My voice isn't the same."

"She's hard of hearing."

"You're pretending all these things!" Elizabeth was dismayed by Lettie's seriousness.

"No, I mean it. If I have to keep seeing her, I know I'll hurt her and end up in prison. She gives me two shillings a week. I can't turn that down. I need it. *We* need it. You share *your* mending work with me. I helped you when you ran the coffee shop. Please, do it once to see if it'll work. You'll get a shilling to show up and hold your hand out."

"You said she questions you and tells you things."

"So, *you* can listen. You know what I do. Answer her questions, take the coins and leave. Just don't let her get a good look at your fingers, Long Liz." Lettie chuckled. She had a playful self-satisfied expression.

Elizabeth wasn't amused, but she would give Lettie's plan a try for the shilling.

Malcolms was Mary's married name. She was a sweater; she rented a room in a tenement and turned it into a workshop, employing children to finish partially completed products provided by a wholesaler. Currently she worked for a manufacturer of ready-made clothing. When Elizabeth arrived at her shop in Red Lion Street, Mary was disciplining a young girl, perhaps eight years old, who had sewn a seam too tight. The punishment involved the girl being stuck in the arm with the needle with which she'd committed the offense. "You'll work the rest of the day for nothing," Mary said, "or you can find other work."

The girl, a cute child with curly brown locks pulled back and tied with a dirty grey ribbon, wiped a spot of blood from her arm, nodded her head, and turned back to her task without complaint.

Perhaps a dozen young girls were gathered in the room, each sitting at a small table, working on a pair of trousers with needle and thread.

Elizabeth was still looking around the room when Mary turned to her. "My guardian angel graces me with her presence, yet again," the woman said bitterly.

Elizabeth could see that Mrs. Malcolms thought she faced her sister.

"Come again for what's due, have you?" Mary walked to a

small desk, opened a drawer and set two coins on the desktop. "And what will you do when I'm gone? Do you ever think about that, Elizabeth?"

Elizabeth stepped back at the sound of her name, thinking that somehow the woman had seen through her ruse. But, no, that was Lettie's name as well.

"Did you work this week," Mary asked her, "or have you been on the blob?"

The woman was horrible. No wonder Lettie hated her. Elizabeth said evenly, "I'm not a beggar. I charred for Reverend Harris Monday and Wednesday, Thursday and Friday I worked at Scab's laundry, and I mended clothes for clients each night. I've been looking for a position within a household. There are precious few to be had."

She thought she'd done a good job mimicking Lettie's voice. When Mrs. Malcolms didn't respond right away, however, Elizabeth began to worry. She remained silent and finally, the woman spoke.

"That's a fine lot of work, if it's true."

Elizabeth held out her hands and risked getting close enough that Mary could see the calloused skin. Elizabeth backed away quickly when Mary looked up.

"Something has changed in you," the woman said.

Again, Elizabeth worried that she'd exposed herself, but she pressed on. "No, I'm no shirkster. I've worked hard for a long time."

"Not that I could tell," Mrs. Malcolms said dismissively. "When was the last time you shared anything with me that I didn't pull out of you?"

Elizabeth had no such difficulties with the woman, and decided she could be as generous as she liked. "I'm sorry I've given you trouble."

Mary folded her arms and smiled. Elizabeth gave her a smile in return.

"Well, I must say," Mary said, "I like the change." She stood a moment longer, staring.

While Elizabeth shrank inside and held her breath for fear that she'd be discovered, she stood tall with a level gaze for Mrs. Malcolms.

Finally, the woman walked to the desk, retrieved the coins, two shillings, and handed them to Elizabeth.

"Thank you, sister," she said.

Mary seemed speechless, her expression wavering between curiosity and consternation.

Elizabeth turned and walked out.

She returned weekly to the same workshop room for more. Each time, Mrs. Malcolms gave her two shillings. Each time, Elizabeth met Lettie afterwards at the corner of Red Lion Street and High Holborn to split the take. Although Elizabeth did not like the sweater much, she established a good, if spurious, rapport with her. She exchanged a few pleasantries with Mrs. Malcolms, answered a few questions, and left somewhat richer. Well worth her effort, the visits took but a few minutes. Over time, when questioned by the woman, Elizabeth told increasingly more of her own experiences instead of those of Lettie. She allowed Mrs. Malcolms to believe that Lettie worked in a coffee shop in Poplar and that folks called her Long Liz. Elizabeth showed a mole on her leg and told Mrs. Malcolms that was where the adder bite had occurred. Elizabeth's history became so mixed up with Lettie's that no doubt Mrs. Malcolms would be unable to distinguish between the two of them.

23

THE LONDON BEAST'S GIZZARD

Despite all their hard work, by 1877, Elizabeth and Jon were able to afford meat only once a week. As their diet suffered, so did their health. In late summer, Jon endured a prolonged case of influenza. He couldn't work for several months, and Elizabeth was having a harder time finding employment of any sort.

She sought help at the Poplar Workhouse. A relieving officer was sent to look in on Jon, to inspect the conditions of the Stride home, and to question Elizabeth about her health and ability to work. After the officer's visit, a nurse was dispatched to attend to Jon briefly on two occasions, and Elizabeth was asked to report to the workhouse to meet the matron, Mrs. Malkwin.

She was a plump, gray-haired woman in her mid-forties with reddened skin on her short neck and round cheeks. In her blue and white uniform, she cut an imposing figure. She spoke to Elizabeth in a matter-of-fact manner. "You will arrive at six o'clock each morning, except for Sundays, for the labor test given in return for relief. I will place you in the needle-room to sew sacks. A subsistence allowance of six shillings, eight pence, and a loaf of bread will be issued to you once a week provided you perform the required labor."

The allowance wasn't enough to live on, but Elizabeth would have to make do somehow. The next day, she arrived at the workhouse at the appointed time.

"Did you bring anything with you besides the clothes you wear?" the matron asked during her admissions inspection.

"Only this," Elizabeth said, taking a metal thimble from her pocket.

"We must all use the leather thimbles that are issued to avoid the appearance that one inmate has an advantage over another," Mrs. Malkwin said.

"No one would have to know," Elizabeth said.

"No secrets are kept here," the matron said sternly. "If one of the other inmates saw you had a metal thimble, she would try to take it from you. I won't allow disruption in the schedule over such pettiness."

Elizabeth knew the many hours of sewing would result in the leather becoming weak and allowing the needle to poke holes in her fingers.

Seeming to anticipate her, Mrs. Malkwin said, "Inmates are issued one leather thimble. You may take it home and repair it as much as you'd like. Once it can no longer be repaired, you are expected to provide your own, a leather one, like that which is issued."

She held out her hand to take the metal thimble, and Elizabeth dropped it in her palm. She did so from sufficient height that it bounced and almost got away from the woman. Mrs. Malkwin clearly saw Elizabeth's defiance in the act. As the matron slipped the thimble into the pocket of her apron, she glared at Elizabeth.

"You'll be trouble if I'm not hard on you," Mrs. Malkwin said. "Instead of working in the needle-room, you'll pick oakum."

Dread of the notoriously grim task took hold of Elizabeth and she regretted her lack of discipline. As she was led to a work station, the matron reminded her that there was no talking allowed. Elizabeth was given a hard wooden seat against a wall with short partitions between herself and female inmate workers on either side. A bundle of rope segments, chopped into ten to twenty inch lengths, was dumped at her feet. The densely spun brown sections were to be carefully unraveled and untangled, each fiber liberated from the others and piled together. Undoing her first length of the rope was not difficult.

The work isn't as bad as you feared, Bess said.

As Elizabeth performed the task repetitively over the course of many hours, reality set in. Sitting for so long on the hard seat was backbreaking, and the labor was an abrasive insult to the flesh of the hands.

She picked two and one half pounds of oakum each day. The task left the skin of her fingers broken and bleeding. The first day, a Monday, twelve hours passed before she'd picked the required amount of oakum.

They want you to suffer, Liza said. *Don't give them satisfaction by showing your misery.*

Each morning when she awoke at home, she was so weary from the day before that she had to work up her courage to go back to the workhouse. Looking at her sleeping husband, lying pale and pitiful beside her in the bed, she'd think about the need to keep him fed. That got her up and moving each time, despite Liza's complaints that he wasn't worth the suffering. Walking to and from the workhouse, she gently rubbed her hands deep into her hair to transfer oil from her scalp to her dry, cracked skin. Saturday of her first week, she succeeded in picking two and a half pounds of oakum in eight hours, which left her enough time to walk to Red Lion Street to gather two shillings from Mary Malcolms.

That Sunday, she could not get out of bed. Although she had told Jon not to get up, he did so to fetch her bread and butter. When she returned home from the workhouse each day after that, she found a simple meal he'd prepared for her, usually slices of bread with a bit of fat spread on them, butter or lard. On two occasions she returned home to find that he'd boiled potatoes. He also prepared warm salt water for her to soak her hands in to toughen them. She knew the difficulty he had getting out of bed. While she protested that she could provide for herself, he was insistent. As the days passed, he had an easier time of it, however. Elizabeth ceased to protest, and enjoyed the care he gave her.

In her second week, she could not contain her complaints any longer and said to Jon, "I understand the workhouse guardians want the work to be a hardship so only the truly needy will ask for relief, but why must they work us until we're miserable?"

"For fear wages will suffer," Jon said, "Parliament doesn't want relief to compete with labor."

"Jobs are so hard to come by, wages drop anyway," Elizabeth said. "There are so many hungry people who'll die without relief."

"There are workhouse Guardians with good intentions. At least once a week, though, I read in the newspaper that some crow or another in Parliament is squawking about how those who bear the harsh treatment deserve it because they lack the moral strength to do better. You know that's the common belief."

Indeed, he was't telling Elizabeth anything she didn't already understand. Working in the coffee shop for so many years, she'd heard plenty of well-dressed people push such ideas about the poor. Most were careful not to sound too heartless. Working with Lettie at laundries and kitchens, she'd noticed the same sort of message was well-received and repeated by many laborers who treated the poor as scapegoats, despite the fact that the workers themselves suffered low wages, long hours, and no redress with employers who had little regard for the needs of those they employed.

Jon shook his head. "As long as people see the poor as

mumpers, prigs, and sharpers, employers will do as they please."

"I'm no thief or con artist!" Elizabeth said. "I don't go to the workhouse because I'm not willing to do better."

"I know," Jon said, gently reaching to take her dry, cracked hands. "You're a hard-working woman."

She remembered that on the day she arrived in London, the city was a great beast trying to digest her. At present, she saw the workhouse as the London beast's gastric mill, a great gizzard full of hard knocks meant to grind the toughness out of those the city might have trouble digesting otherwise. She was determined not to let it beat her, but feared she would soon meet her limit.

Elizabeth had seen one woman go mad while picking oakum. The poor creature had dropped her work, abruptly stood at her station, and begun screaming and flailing as if she were caught in a net. Then she'd bitten her own hands as if trying to eat them. She severed two fingers before she was stopped and hauled away, wailing her heart out.

Jon placed a hand on Elizabeth's cheek and said, "I will be back to work soon."

The frequency and severity of his coughing diminished during her third week of workhouse out-relief and he had more color than in recent days past. In her fourth week, Jon was feeling much stronger, and started looking for work.

At the beginning of her fifth week, because she had caused Mrs. Malkwin no grief since handing over her thimble nearly a month earlier, Elizabeth was placed in the needle-room. As she worked, sewing sacks, holes appeared in the leather thimble she was given. Elizabeth repositioned the device numerous times to protect her fingers. Inevitably, she poked several holes in her fingertip. She was relieved at the end of the week to hear that Jon had found work, helping to build scaffolding for the new law court under construction in Fleet Street.

Elizabeth rested for three days. She was relieved that she and Jon had both survived. Although she had hope for their future, it occurred to her that the notion of something better was a thing of the past. On the fourth day after quitting the Poplar Workhouse, she took temporary work at Scab's laundry where Lettie was working.

In 1878, the Strides moved into an old three room house in Usher Road already shared by two other families. They occupied the smallest room toward the rear of the dwelling and had to pass through the living areas of the other families when coming and going from home. Thankfully, the Levine family, a husband, wife, and two children, and the Burkins, a mother and daughter, did not begrudge the Strides access day or night.

Having no permanent work and temporary work harder to find, Elizabeth spent increasing amounts of her spare time learning to beg on the streets. She didn't tell Jon about what she was doing. She took a beat along the edges of Victoria Park and asked for assistance from passersby. The take was hardly worth the effort at first. She dressed in her oldest, most worn clothing, dirtied her face and hands, and allowed her hair to become a mess.

Most beggars she encountered gave each other a wide berth, perhaps out of sympathy. Some who were territorial, however, gave her the evil eye or vocal warnings. Elizabeth was chased away from one corner by an immense man wearing women's clothing and playing a penny whistle. Strangely, she found the incident exciting. Something about keeping her activities a secret and the danger involved was appealing.

Life has enough hazards as it is, Liza warned. *Don't look for pleasure in risk.*

Elizabeth took the warning seriously for fear that if something happened to her, Jon would be left to fend for himself.

She befriended a thin, bedraggled woman named Poppy, who

seemed harmless. Each day, Poppy sat in the park beside the path that passed over Regents Canal to Approach Road. She wore clothing in such disrepair that much of her arms and legs were exposed.

"You don't know what you're doing," Poppy said, and Elizabeth agreed with her. "First thing you need to know is to beware the lurkers. They pretend to be beggars, but they're *family people.*"

Elizabeth frowned to show her lack of understanding.

"Criminals," Poppy explained. She described several individuals. "Some are dangerous, all cause us trouble."

"I've seen some of them," Elizabeth said.

"Just stay well away from them. What you need to get on as a mumper is a fakement. You have few choices, since you don't want to take away from someone else."

Again, Elizabeth showed her confusion.

"We earn coin through pity," Poppy said impatiently. She gestured toward her threadbare clothing. "I work the shallow. Mary, with the bruises and broken fingers..." She gestured down the path toward the southeast. "...uses the scaldrums dodge."

Poppy stood and held Elizabeth by the arms, turned her this way and that, taking a good look. "You've got the crooked leg, but I'd say you'd be a glim. I haven't seen any use that for a while. All you need is charcoal or lamp black to help you look as though you got burned out. You rub the black into you clothes, your skin and hair, maybe pinch yourself to look scorch red." She paused and looked Elizabeth in the eye. "Or just go on the blob. Write a hard luck story on a board and carry it around."

You could pretend to be a survivor of the Princess Alice, Liza suggested.

Elizabeth nodded and thanked Poppy.

At home, she rummaged for a short section of board among the scraps of wood Jon kept. She chose one she thought he wouldn't miss. Using some of his black paint and a lettering brush, she wrote on the board in her best script a short statement that read, "Lost husband and two children to the Princess Alice. Now destitute."

More than six-hundred people had died when the Princess Alice, a moonlight excursion vessel, collided with the collier, Bywell Castle, in September, less than a month earlier. Most of those who perished were passengers enjoying the evening pleasure cruise. The people Elizabeth encountered on her beat who knew someone involved, or at least had heard of someone associated with the tragedy, were sympathetic.

When Poppy saw Elizabeth's board one afternoon, she gave a knowing smile and nodded her approval.

As her technique improved, so did her income. The earnings were not nearly as good as working a job for a wage.

Elizabeth received a package sent from the address to which she'd written to her father. In it was a Swedish hymn book and a letter from her sister, Kristina, telling of her father's death. Elizabeth didn't know how she felt about the news. She cherished the book. Although none within her family were devout members of the Swedish Church, they had all sung songs from the book together, and having a copy of the hymnal gave her a nostalgia for the security of her early life. She wrote to Kristina to thank her. The letter was the first of a monthly effort to communicate by post with her sister. She never heard back from Kristina, though, and wasn't certain her messages were being received.

Elizabeth continued to see her twin once a week to share the two shillings collected from Mary Malcolms. "How are you and Jon faring?" Lettie asked, but because she appeared distracted by her own problems of finding work, paying her rent, and feeding herself, Elizabeth didn't tell her a sad tale.

With few carpentry jobs to be had, and difficulty doing the work when it did come, Jon offered furniture mending and found a few customers. He repaired weak joints in legs, rungs, rails, backs, and panels of various types of furnishings and he wove chair seats. His income was small. Hours of sitting further deteriorated his back and by 1880, he was capable of working half the hours he'd been able to work a year earlier.

Elizabeth applied for medical assistance for Jon at the Poplar Workhouse and a relief officer was again sent to look in on the Strides' home life.

After an interview with Jon and Elizabeth, the officer, a gentleman named Edwards, said to Elizabeth, "With back pain and rheumatism, your husband isn't presently in danger and so out-relief medical assistance in your home is not prescribed. Inmate relief is not justified since you are able-bodied."

"He suffers such that he *cannot* work most of the time," Elizabeth said, "and I can't find enough work to keep him."

"I'm sorry," Mr. Edwards said, "there is the labor test for a subsistence allowance. You are certainly fit for—"

"No!" Elizabeth said, cutting him off. A shudder ran through her with the memory of her days in the workhouse. "It's not enough."

"I'm sorry I can't help you," Mr. Edwards said. He made his way out through the living quarters of the Burkins and Levine families.

"We will get by, Elizabeth," Jon said. "I'm not done just yet."

Elizabeth feared that was not true. Her worries for Jon's wellbeing followed her everywhere.

In the winter of 1881, Elizabeth went to see the clerk at the Swedish Church, a gentleman named Olsson, to appeal for alms. He provided her with four shillings on two occasions.

"I cannot help you further at this time," he said the third time she asked for help. "We have many unfortunates within our parish, particularly those with children, who need the help more. I'm sorry."

When Elizabeth complained about the clerk's decision, Jon shook his head slowly. Elizabeth had brought him his supper: A slice of bread. He could no longer work and had taken to bed several weeks earlier. Propped up on their mattress, he ate, while she sat in a chair beside him, having her own slice.

"You spend all your time trying to keep me," he said. "Daily, I take your life away from you."

"No," Elizabeth said, "that's *not* true."

"If you didn't have to struggle for my sake," he said, "you wouldn't go hungry, you would have an easier time finding and keeping work, and you could begin your life anew."

"I will *not* leave you," Elizabeth said. "You are my husband!"

"They will take care of me at the workhouse infirmary if you leave me. As long as you're here, they won't."

"No," Elizabeth said, "You cannot *live* in the workhouse."

"I cannot *live* out here," he said sadly. He was silent for a time as if thinking something through.

"I'm doing the best I can," Elizabeth said.

"Well—" he paused as if a regret had taken hold of him, but then he blundered forward. "—it's not enough. You're doing a poor job of it and I can't take it anymore. Leave me, so I can receive the care I need."

Elizabeth looked at him in horror. Had he ceased to love her?

"You're not a good wife," he shouted hoarsely. "I've suffered at your hands, and now I would have out of this cruel marriage."

His trembling lips and the tears that slid from his eyes gave him away.

Elizabeth knelt beside the bed and touched his face. "I know you don't mean it," she said.

He gathered her into his arms and wept, his frail body shuddering with the effort. "I'm sorry, sweet woman. I must do what I have to. I *am* suffering and so are *you*."

Elizabeth sobbed against his shoulder. She knew he spoke the truth.

Elizabeth left Jon within the week, and on his behalf applied for invalid relief from the Poplar Workhouse. Again, the relief officer came to the house in Usher Road. Elizabeth wasn't there to hear the interview.

She found a room in a doss house in Bow Road not far away, where she shared a bed with six to eight strangers. By the time she arrived each night one or more of her bedmates had already stripped the bedclothes and nearly worthless mattress off the bed frame to avoid contact with vermin. Elizabeth slept in her clothing on the hard bed boards. Fearing robbery from her bedmates, invariably strangers, she slept with a knife tucked into her bodice.

Elizabeth was fending for herself within the gut of the London beast again. The hardship was worthwhile, she decided, as long as Jon received the care he needed. She would improve her own situation as soon as she could.

The next time she saw Jon was in the evening, two days after his admittance to the infirm male ward of the Poplar Workhouse. The room housed at least thirty men, the beds separated by curtains. The place reeked of human excrement, the odor seeming to come from a small alcove in one corner of the ward. No doubt the privy was backed up.

Although bedridden, Jon was in good spirits. His scalp shown white as a skull through the terrier crop they'd given his hair, and that was disturbing to see, yet he looked to be reasonably well fed.

"Once again, your sweet face brightens my day, Elizabeth," he said.

She smiled crookedly and sat on the edge of his bed.

"What will you do?" he asked. "Where will you go?"

They had been over the subject several times, but his memory wasn't what it had been.

"I've gone to a four-penny hotel."

He had the same reaction. "No, I don't want you in a common lodging."

She tried something new. "I'll beg Lettie to take me in."

"Who?"

"Lettie," Elizabeth said, thinking he hadn't heard. He shook his head slowly, and she tried again. "Elizabeth—Elizabeth Sneller."

Still the name seemed to mean nothing to him. Elizabeth realized that Lettie had rarely, if ever, been around when Jon was home. When her twin had married Mr. Sneller, Jon had been away on a carpentry job. She decided that his memory had simply failed him again.

"Lettie—I mean Elizabeth—introduced us in Hyde Park."

"Nobody introduced us. Was the wind that brought us together. A breeze blew your bonnet off. I retrieved it and we struck up a conversation."

Of little importance, Elizabeth let the matter go. Over the next few hours, she had such a pleasant time, talking with Jon and exchanging news, that she lost track of the time. A nurse noticed her at ten o'clock in the evening.

"How did we not see you there?" the woman said with a frown. "Visiting hours were over at eight o'clock. I locked the doors at nine. Up and out or you'll have to spend the night in the foul ward."

Jon made a look of mock fear. "Oh, they've got pox of all sorts in there."

"That's right," the nurse said, maintaining her stern expression.

"You've done your time in the spike, my dear," Jon said. "Now, go!"

Elizabeth knew he was teasing her, but the urgency of his last words left her uneasy. She didn't want to leave him, but she got up quickly, made her goodbyes, and fled, a fear of becoming trapped in the workhouse snapping at her heels. She was relieved when the large wooden door banged shut behind her and she heard a key turn in the lock.

She was allowed to visit each day. Having to earn a crust, though, kept her away much of the time.

On the evening of October 23, 1884, she tried to visit Jon at the Poplar Workhouse, only to be informed that he had been taken to the sick asylum, Bromley, a short walk away. Elizabeth arrived to find Jon fading in and out of consciousness. His pulse was weak. The nurses tried to go about their business as usual, yet when they saw Elizabeth sitting beside Jon's bed, holding his hand, they either turned away quickly or tried to give her a sympathetic smile. Elizabeth knew they had no hope for Jon.

"You are young," Jon said, startling her. Until the present, he'd given no indication that he noticed Elizabeth, and her thoughts had wandered. "Find another man to love you. Allow that sweet face to brighten another fellow's day. You've been a good wife to me and I love you for it."

Elizabeth hugged his hand to her face and held back her tears.

"We're closing for the night," the attending nurse said. "You can come back tomorrow."

Elizabeth didn't want to leave. She would have risked becoming trapped in the workhouse. The nurse stood with her arms crossed over her chest, however. There would be no arguing with her.

Elizabeth turned to her husband. "I love you, Jon."

"That's made all the difference in my life," he said.

Elizabeth looked into his tired eyes and smiled the best she could.

He is not long for this world, Liza said. *You had better start looking for another—*

Shut up! Elizabeth thought. In that moment she hated her cynical voice.

If you hurry, Bess said, *he will still be here tomorrow.*

Distraught and unsteady, but not wanting to upset Jon, Elizabeth released him and walked away as quickly as she dared.

©2014

24

DECISION

Following Jon's death, Elizabeth found temporary work scouring pots and pans at the Beehive Tavern in Whitechapel. She went to live with her twin in Brick Lane. Lettie's room was bright yellow, and had a small window about a foot across that looked west toward the street. Being a second floor room, there was no need to curtain the window to keep folks from seeing in. Late in the afternoon, sunlight streamed through the rectangle of dirty glass and seemed to set the yellow room on fire.

Until Elizabeth came, Lettie was having problems paying the rent. Between the two of them, Elizabeth begging on the street, collecting the two shillings per week from Mary Malcolms, and working at the Beehive, and Lettie working at Peterkin's Laundry, they scrounged up the funds for November's rent.

At the beginning of December, Elizabeth's luck ran out. Her work at the Beehive was given to someone else, and she started looking elsewhere for employment. She found nothing that would provide the needed funds in time. Following hours of looking for work, she sat in a pub in the afternoon eating bread and cheese. The yeasty smell of the place got into her nose and made her thirst for ale. Frightened, she tried to reason with the yearning. She was no good when she drank. A glass of ale would cost one of her precious pennies. She wouldn't be able to look for work with the smell on her breath. Still, she wouldn't have to eat as much if she got the ale in her, and her troubles would evaporate for a time. Elizabeth decided she could have one glass and no more.

After the first glass, negotiations with the urge for the second and third were progressively shorter. Then, she stumbled out into the street, resolved to find a client to pay her for sex.

"Fancy a bit of wagtail," she said to a young fellow in a new suit, standing out front of the pub. She did a little dance to wiggle her backside. The man turned and walked away.

Elizabeth had never done solicitation on the street before. As drunk as she was, after so long without alcohol, she had no sense of how loud her words were or how obvious were her actions. Most of the men she approached were disgusted or simply amused.

One fellow grabbed roughly for her breasts. "Sure, I'll have your bubbies," he said, laughing. When he gripped her arm painfully, she broke away and ran. He didn't follow.

Eventually, a constable appeared and took her to the Commercial Road police station. Since she was unfamiliar to the police, she was allowed to sleep off her drunkenness in a cell. She received a warning, and she was released that evening.

The shame Elizabeth felt for her behavior emerged as the effect of the alcohol wore off. She was mortified as she spoke to Lettie about the events of the day late that night.

Listening to the account, her twin was clearly upset, but she was quiet for some time when Elizabeth was done.

Finally, Lettie took a deep breath and said, "Mr. Snopes has asked me to marry him." She had been courting the man for over a month, yet Elizabeth didn't think Lettie took the relationship very seriously. "He wants us to live here because it's better than his room. I didn't know what to say to you about it, and I've been putting him off because I know you have nowhere else to go."

Again, she was quiet for a time, and Elizabeth was dreading what would come next.

"But I've decided I want to accept his proposal, and I have to ask you to find another place to live."

"I have no work," Elizabeth protested. "You would not have been able to pay this month if I hadn't provided so much help."

"Yes, and that's the point, isn't it?" Lettie said. "I can't make the nethers by myself, and you currently haven't the income to help."

"I could make a pallet on the floor," Elizabeth said quickly, "and Mr. Snopes can have my place in the bed."

"You know he won't want you here, especially since..." She paused, obviously unwilling to say that he wouldn't want a prostitute in his home. "Surely, you understand."

The woman has merely used you all these years, Liza said. *Since you no longer have work she can share, you are merely in her way. When—*

"No, I don't understand," Elizabeth said, cutting off the hateful voice. She would not have such things said about her twin, even though she suspected there was some truth to them. "I thought we were sisters, that we shared everything."

Lettie's face turned dark. "You don't expect me to *share* my husband, do you?"

"No, but I don't know where I'll go." Elizabeth was embarrassed by the desperation in her voice.

"You've slept in the four-penny hotel before."

"I stayed in a doss house as a last resort. Do you know what they're like?"

Lettie didn't answer. Her face became expressionless, her eyes impenetrable.

Elizabeth stared at her for a time, as she strained toward understanding.

"I'm sorry," Lettie said, finally. "If you were in my place, you'd do the same to get on." She got up, wrapped a shawl around her shoulders and walked out the door. Elizabeth heard Lettie's footsteps moving down the tenement stairs, and the door that led to the outside opening and closing.

And Elizabeth *did* understand. Survival took priority over all other considerations. Still, the two women had helped each other for so long, she couldn't help seeing her twin's choice as betrayal.

As she had done numerous times before, Elizabeth sat and watched the afternoon sunlight that came through the small window of the room creep across the wall. Although the light and color in the yellow room were beautiful, the lateness of the hour and the melancholy of another day ending always conspired to give Elizabeth the sense that her chance at life had passed away with Jon. For a few days following his death, she'd felt something akin to hunger pangs, but of the heart, not the stomach. If she could hold him, kiss him, tell him that he was loved one more time, she would become full again. Unsatisfied, however, her heart seemed to wither and she felt hollow inside. At present, she feared that if she did not act, all that was left for her was the temporary warm sunset of memory, to be followed by a long night of regret. She had no time for such foolishness. She must do as Jon told her and find another man. Again, she must find something better.

She got up, packed her things, including her Swedish hymnal, and left.

Elizabeth went to stay at a common lodging house at 32 Flower and Dean Street. She paid to have a few of her possessions, including the Swedish hymnal, stored under lock and key in the doss house.

On the Saturday evening after leaving the yellow room for the last time, she went, as usual, to collect two shillings from Mary Malcolms. Afterward, as Elizabeth walked to the place where she would meet Lettie and split the take, she wondered if her twin would show up. She wasn't certain whether she preferred her twin to be there or for her to stay away. Since coming to Whitechapel, Elizabeth had met with Lettie at the corner of Commercial and Quaker Streets. Lettie was usually late, yet she was standing on the corner when Elizabeth got there.

"You should continue to see my sister each Saturday," Lettie said, "if you would."

"Yes," Elizabeth said. Unwilling to offer anything more to the conversation, she turned and walked away.

At their subsequent meetings, Elizabeth often remained silent as she handed her estranged twin a shilling. With time, a sadness appeared in Lettie's eyes that Elizabeth hoped was regret. She missed her friend, but her pride kept her from speaking.

In her ongoing search for employment, Elizabeth found only sporadic, temporary work.

Out of necessity, she became much better at soliciting. For all her reasonable dread, she also found an unreasonable excitement in the pursuit.

You foolishly felt excitement over the risks of begging too, Liza said.

There are no opportunities without risk, Bess said.

Elizabeth considered the statement uncharacteristically mature for her innocent voice.

Perhaps, Liza said, *but it's unhealthy to seek danger.*

Since Elizabeth's primary purpose was to find a man to help provide her with something better than nights in a doss house and days on the street, her approach to soliciting became more subtle. She offered sex for a price only if she thought a gentleman would not be offering anything better. Using that tactic, she found Mr. Kidney, a dockside laborer, and ended up in his bed in the summer of 1885. Since he seemed to have a bit of money, buying her drinks at a pub and a good meal at a tavern, she hadn't proposed a fee for her services with the hope that becoming his lover might prove a more effective way of opening his wallet. He got drunk with her, and invited her to stay for several days in his room in a tenement in Dorset Street, which seemed much nicer than anything she would have expected of a dockside laborer.

The chamber, accessed through a hallway entrance at the front of the tenement, had two windows that faced the street front of the building. Wallpaper, incorporating burgundy-colored silk ribbons in its design, decorated the walls. A fine armoire and five-drawer set rested against the southwest wall and a bedside cupboard and small vanity sat against the northeast wall. The iron bed was painted blue and had a feather mattress. Elizabeth had the impression that the room was more suited for a woman. Mr. Kidney was away at work all day, and when he returned from his labors each evening, their romps in bed continued. They seemed to get along together quite naturally.

"Do you think you'd like to stay here?" he asked on their fourth evening together.

"I am already here," she said happily, hoping he would offer more.

"I'm asking you to come here to live. I'll keep you comfortable and well-fed."

Elizabeth could not believe her luck. Almost ten years younger than she was, he was strong, tall, and handsome, with a great curling mustache and a head full of thick, wavy hair. She'd told him she was thirty-five years old, six year younger than her true age, and he'd seemed to accept that.

He's a cash— Liza began.

Resentfully, Elizabeth cut her off. "Yes," she said quickly, throwing her arms around him and laughing as they rolled together in bed.

When her expression of delight had subsided, he propped himself up on a pillow and lit a cigarette. "My last twist, she died rather sudden, run down in the road by a toff in his landau," he said, as if the information was somehow pertinent to their discussion. Elizabeth didn't know what to make of it.

"Working at the docks, I meet all sorts of men, fresh off their ships, asking for girls. I'm a good judge of character, no matter where they come from, and will provide you with only the best clients."

All that she thought she'd known about the man fled in an instant as she looked at him. With the sudden thought that he was Klaudio, she recoiled in shock, falling backwards out of the bed and striking her head on the floor.

Mr. Kidney helped her up. She wasn't so addled by the blow that she didn't know who he was and what had happened. He wasn't Klaudio, but her initial reaction was that he might as well be. While she was working on turning him into a lover, he'd been grooming her to become an employee.

Mr. Kidney had seen through her from the start, or at least had an intuition that she was receptive to engaging in prostitution. *Is it that obvious?* Elizabeth shrank inside from the knowledge that her character was so easily read.

You don't want to regret not hearing from me, Liza said.

Elizabeth begrudgingly accepted the truth presented by her cynical voice. Mr. Kidney was indeed a cash carrier.

Question him, Liza said.

"That was quite a tumble," Mr. Kidney said, gently touching the back of her head. "Did you crack your loaf?"

Elizabeth shook her head. She had a decision to make. Once she'd composed herself, she asked, "How many girls do you have?"

"I keep one at a time," he said. "Since she's my Judy as well, I keep her safe. Clients come here only when I'm out."

For a ponce, Mr. Kidney was not a bad sort, Elizabeth decided. He would introduce her to a lot of men over time. Possibly, the man who would provide for her in years to come would be aboard one of the ships he met at the docks.

When you meet that man in the future, Bess said, *he'll carry you away from London to his home abroad, perhaps to something better in a new place, like America.*

"I can see that you didn't understand," Mr. Kidney said.

Elizabeth turned to him, looked him in the eyes, and shook her head dismissively. "Not at all," she lied. "Yes, I would like to stay."

Elizabeth assumed Liza would have something more to say, yet she was strangely quiet.

Elizabeth moved her few possessions from the doss house in Flower and Dean Street to Mr. Kidney's room. While with him, Elizabeth saw no more than one client per day. She required them to wear vulcanized rubber sheaths when having sexual intercourse with her. Preferring the "buttered bun," as he referred to it, Mr. Kidney most often mounted her within an hour after she'd finished with a client. She received no pay for her services, but was kept well-fed and comfortable in Mr. Kidney's room. She did, however, occasionally receive a small gratuity from a client, which she hid away for future use. The days and weeks bled together.

25

ARGUMENTS

"Do you want to find another girl?" Elizabeth asked Mr. Kidney defiantly.

Liza had coached her on what to say to the man. While she dreaded the words of her cynical voice, she knew she must hear them for her own protection.

"No," he said, "but if you cause me more trouble, I'll have to consider it."

"You made the mistake of telling me about how difficult it was to find me."

"My need *is* particular." Mr. Kidney's frown was too awkward to read clearly.

He'd grown up in a whore house. His predilection was for older women who were very much used. He did, in fact, prefer to have sexual intercourse with a woman who had been lubricated by copulation with another man.

"Therefore," Elizabeth said, "if you want me to do your

bidding, you'll have to allow me to blow off steam from time to time."

The night before she'd had a sudden need to get away. She'd stood up the client Mr. Kidney was sending to their room, and merely walked out the door to get drunk at the Blue Coat Boy Pub next door. She'd exited the pub after several glasses of ale and become a nuisance on the street, accosting the men going in and out of the establishment. Elizabeth was arrested for public drunkenness and Mr. Kidney had to fetch her from the jail.

"Yet you must be reliable," he said.

"Haven't I been? I've been with you almost a year."

"Until now, yes."

"No matter how comfortable you make the cage, it's still a cage unless I can get out when I please."

"I understand your need, and only ask that you let me know when you want to be away so my reputation doesn't suffer."

"I will," Elizabeth said, but she instantly knew she would not. Experiencing his disappointment and not suffering any consequences had just become an important affirmation of her independence.

Thankfully, Mr. Kidney was not Klaudio. Her employer's need left him vulnerable to her whims. After nearly a year of seeing the caliber of the men he sent to her, Elizabeth knew he would never find her a man who would do her any good. If she wanted to find one who would provide her with something better than the life she led, she'd have to discover him herself.

Elizabeth slipped out periodically to wander the streets of Whitechapel and carouse for days on end. Each time, she experienced the excitement of not knowing what she'd find; the good, the bad or the indifferent. Although she told herself she was looking for a man, she spent most her time away drunk, and was occasionally jailed for public drunkenness. She used various ways to explain away her drunken behavior when required to answer for it. Her slurred speech was the result of damage to the roof of her mouth incurred during her struggle to survive the sinking of the Princess Alice. Once, she was released from jail because she told the sergeant at the police station that she was subject to epileptic fits.

"You may have all the fits you like," was his response.

"When I have a spell," she said pitifully, "if someone isn't near to place something wooden in my mouth, I might bite my tongue and bleed to death. It could happen very quickly."

The sergeant thought about that for a moment, then gave her a warning and sent her on her way.

The length of her binges increased with time to several weeks, during which she stayed in the common lodging in Flower and Dean Street. To those she met, she was simply Long Liz, a woman who had lost her husband and children in the Princess Alice disaster. Her forays were often cut short because she spent some of her funds feeding acquaintances from the doss house who were elderly and obviously undernourished. Since her experience with Jon, she had a soft spot for those growing old and infirm. She also owed a debt to the elderly for her treatment of Fru Andersdotter.

Bess's notions of hope emerged most warmly and powerfully with drink. While Liza's warnings continued to help her avoid danger, Elizabeth often wanted to shut out the cynical words. She was particularly vulnerable to them when hung over. Following each binge, Liza warned, *Besotted with ale, you'll never find the man you seek.*

During one roaring drunk, Bess and Liza became more for Elizabeth than mere voices. She was returning to the common lodging house in Flower and Dean Street when she slipped and fell in a refuse pile outside the kitchen door of the Beehive Tavern.

Get up, Liza said, *before someone comes along and nobbles you.*

Most of the customers coming and going through the entrance to the establishment, some fifty feet away, avoided looking in her direction.

Nobody would bother to harm me, she thought. Still, she felt a tugging at her left arm as if Liza were trying to pull her away. Looking in that direction, though, Elizabeth saw no one.

The warmth of a recently dumped pot of spoiled pease pottage amidst the refuse felt good against her backside.

Since you're already down, Bess said, *you might as well enjoy the warmth until it's gone.*

Despite knowing that her skirts would be caked with filth when she stood, Elizabeth liked Bess's suggestion. She sensed a comforting presence to her right, though, again, there was no one there.

You wallow in the London beast offal! Liza spat. *Listening to that child, you'll end up at the morgue. What good has she ever done you? She helps you hide from the truth at every turn.*

Elizabeth was outraged to hear the anger in Liza's voice. She'd never considered that her voices might not get along, let alone that one might bear resentment toward the other. How dare Liza lash out at Bess that way? Elizabeth intended to defend the innocent child and scold her cynical voice, yet Bess beat her to it.

You want to talk about truth—she might still have her Jon now, if you'd allowed her to share the truth with him from the start. The trouble in their marriage put him in an early grave!

Elizabeth had never heard Bess speak in anger, but apparently she held resentment as well.

None of it made any sense. "You're not alive!" Elizabeth cried. "You have no opinion that's not my own."

As drunk as she was, the words came out in a guttural ejaculation of drowned vowels and soggy consonants. At the tail end of her words, someone from the kitchen looked to be stepping out for a smoke. Elizabeth recognized her. She was a scourer named Margaret. When Elizabeth had worked at the Beehive Tavern, she'd known and liked the woman. Seeing Elizabeth wallowing in the filth, Margaret put away her pipe, retreated back inside, and shut the door.

While Liza and Bess both spoke the truth, Elizabeth held the most bitterness for her cynical voice. "You kept me from the man I loved," she slurred. "You told me to hide the truth from him. Think of the years of lost love, how much better it all could have been!"

A man in ragged clothes, an unfortunate, approached along the side of the building. Looking for food amongst the kitchen refuse, at first he ignored Elizabeth and she, him.

How many of my warnings have you ignored? Liza asked. *You kept the truth from Jon because you couldn't face it.*

The unfortunate had taken an interest in the warm food beneath Elizabeth, and began pulling her off the pease pottage. Elizabeth confused his grasp for that of the hateful Liza, and flailed to get loose.

Klaudio and his friend, Robert, would not have taken advantage of you if you'd listened to me, Liza spat. *The ponce had already tricked you once when I warned you again. You thought you'd caught Robert's eye. He was going to carry you off to England and a new life. Hortense died because of your choice.*

Elizabeth lashed out, trying to find Liza's black tongue and tear it loose.

How much punishment do you deserve for that? the cynical voice cried. *Must you treat yourself to more neglect than you gave the old woman? How much danger must you face now to assuage the guilt you feel?*

Elizabeth balled her fist and hurled it at Liza, but found herself striking the man hauling her out of the trash. She landed a blow to his face that stunned her hand.

He lifted his fist and swung at her head.

Elizabeth awoke in her bed. She didn't know how long she'd

been insensible. The last two teeth on the left side of her lower jaw were missing. She was miserable and ashamed.

Mr. Kidney spent a week nursing her back to health before allowing her to see clients.

Elizabeth had to admit that if she'd done as Liza had suggested and got out of the refuse beside the Beehive Tavern kitchen, she would have avoided harm. She wouldn't accept the idea, however, that she tried to settle with her conscience for the death of the old woman by putting herself in danger.

Still, she remembered Liza's words from the time when she accepted Mr. Kidney's invitation to live with him: *You don't want to regret not hearing from me.* Although she had come to hate her cynical voice, for Elizabeth's own self-preservation, she made a promise to herself: *If Bess offers advice, I will also always listen to what Liza has to say about it before deciding what's best.*

Elizabeth and Mr. Kidney had many a row about her periodic escapes, one in April of 1887 coming to physical violence. He'd struck her in the face several times and ripped the earring from her left ear, tearing open the lobe. Elizabeth reported to the police at the Commercial Street station that Mr. Kidney had assaulted her, but when time for the hearing came, she was on another of her benders. Since she failed to show up at the Thames Magistrate Court, the charges against him were dropped.

She would stay with him for another year and five months.

26

ESCAPE

Tuesday, September 25, 1888

After a row with Mr. Kidney about his desire to fatten her a bit, Elizabeth made another escape from the room they shared. Before she left, she considered that she might not come back to him, and decided to leave her Swedish hymnal with the woman living next door, a Mrs. Smith. Elizabeth told the woman she would eventually return for it.

She went to the common lodging at 32 Flower and Dean Street. No beds were available at the time. She was directed to the doss house next door, at number 33, owned by the same proprietor, a man named Satchell.

Elizabeth drank little as she made her nightly rounds of several public houses that week, seeking single men. She was finally making an effort to find the man Jon wanted her to have.

Moving through the grim environment of Whitechapel,

she looked to Bess to provide her with hope. While Elizabeth dutifully listened to her cynical voice, she wasn't looking forward to hearing what she had to say. Liza saw nothing but trouble in the world. By her estimation, no good existed for Elizabeth without exposure to extreme danger and inevitable pain.

During the day, Elizabeth took pity on several hungry acquaintances at the doss house and bought them meals. She was low on funds and went to Mrs. Malcolms on Thursday, September 27 to get her shillings early. The woman gave her the coins after a brief argument.

Elizabeth moved back to the doss house at 32 Flower and Dean Street Thursday night because she knew more people there and that diminished the likelihood of having to sleep in beds with complete strangers.

When Saturday came, as usual, Elizabeth met with her twin at the corner of Commercial and Quaker Streets. Lettie had a troubled look.

"I worry about you out working the streets," she said.

Elizabeth shook her head—Lettie obviously didn't understand the situation.

"You've heard about the Whitechapel Murderer?" Lettie asked.

Elizabeth had heard about the murders and speculations about who was responsible. *He's a bit of bad meat in the entrails of London*, she thought. *It'll pass soon.*

She didn't respond to her twin's question.

"Please be careful."

Again, Elizabeth didn't respond. She'd heard about the killings. Still, she couldn't believe the murderer's attention might fix on her.

Lettie is preying upon your fear to get something she wants, Liza said.

Elizabeth had no idea what her twin might want from her, but decided she didn't want Lettie to have any hold over her.

"I won't be going to your sister anymore," Elizabeth said. She held out her hand to give to Lettie all of what remained of the money retrieved from Mrs. Malcolms on Thursday, almost two shillings.

Lettie looked at Elizabeth evenly for a long time before reaching out to take the money. When several coins dropped into Lettie's hand, she seemed confused and then sad, yet she tried to smile. "I'm hungry," she said, touching her stomach. "Would you like to do a tightener?"

What she wants is for you to forgive her, Liza said, as if that were a horrible motive.

Yes, she wants you to forgive her, Bess said, making the idea sound appealing.

Although Elizabeth tried to open her mouth to say yes, somehow she couldn't do it. She blamed Liza, even though the voice had never had control over Elizabeth's person, let alone her decisions. The silence between the women stretched on.

"I'm sorry," Lettie said at last. She paused before saying carefully, "There's something you've wanted to tell me for a long time, something that troubles you. I would hear it without judgment."

If there was anybody Elizabeth might have told about the old woman, Lettie was the one, but the opportunity was gone.

Again, Lettie stood regarding her twin for some time.

While Elizabeth missed sharing a life with her friend, her pride was still too big to swallow, and her shame a wall too high to scale. She pressed her lips together firmly and maintained a chilly gaze.

Finally, Lettie turned away and began walking.

When she was gone, Elizabeth's eyes grew warm, then stung with heat. Tears spilled as she headed back to the doss house.

Late in the afternoon, Elizabeth worked for Mrs. Tanner, the deputy of the common lodging, cleaning two rooms for sixpence. With Mrs. Tanner's help, Elizabeth got her possessions out of the doss house's locked storeroom because her funds were too low to continue paying the storage fee.

Preparing for the evening, Elizabeth washed up at a basin in one of the empty rooms. As she scrubbed herself with a moist flannel, Liza spoke to her. *Lettie is right about the threat in the East End. Flirting with danger isn't the same as seeking a man. You should stay in until the threat has passed.*

I seek only happenstance, Elizabeth thought. *I've happened upon good men; Herr Rikhardsson, Herr Olovsson, Herr Kirschner, Mr. Pimberton, and Jon Stride. I wasn't looking for any of them and still they found me. Would you have me retreat from the world and miss all opportunities?*

An opportunist at heart, Liza was unable to argue further.

Elizabeth dressed in her best: A black skirt, brown velveteen bodice, and a long black jacket, trimmed with fur—all clothing Mr. Kidney had bought for her over time. The clothes were indeed her finest, although she'd worn them so much, they'd become a bit threadbare. No one would notice from a distance. Close up, especially at night, the dark coloration of the fabrics would help hide their condition.

Elizabeth asked one of the women she'd fed earlier in the week to keep certain items that she didn't want to carry with her. On the street, she bought a red rose clutched within a frond of maiden hair fern from a flower girl.

A certain gentleman she'd seen across crowded taverns and pubs had caught her attention over the last few days. She'd yet to meet and speak with him, but his eyes had shown his interest in her. He'd smiled at her twice. Then, when she'd moved toward him, he'd become lost in the crowd and she'd missed him. As she walked to The Hoop and Grapes pub, where she'd last seen the man, she had a feeling she'd finally meet up with him.

27

THE CLIENT

September 29, 1888

Elizabeth was sipping a glass of ale at half-past seven in the evening when two drunken women began drawing attention to themselves. One of the women looked familiar. Elizabeth couldn't quite place her. The management of The Hoop and Grapes pub was tolerant of their antics at first. When the women began upsetting furniture and throwing glasses, they were put out.

Elizabeth finished her ale and decided to move on. When she stepped out of the establishment, she found a crowd had gathered to watch someone running up and down in the middle of Aldgate High Street, shouting and whistling and spitting. The woman was one of the drunkards who had caused trouble inside, the one that seemed familiar to Elizabeth. The other woman was nowhere to be seen. People clustered on the footway on either side of the street were laughing as they watched the drunkard run up and down the road, but Elizabeth couldn't make out why at first. The woman huffed and puffed and spit some more. "Clang, Clang, Clang," she yelled, warning folks out of her way.

Elizabeth smiled, realizing the drunkard was imitating a steam-powered fire engine. Simultaneously, she knew why the woman was familiar. Elizabeth had seen her earlier that summer, crouched among crates in an alley, playing Grandmother's Trunk with an unseen companion. Clearly, the poor creature was mad.

Remembering the woman talking to her imaginary opponent during her game in the alley, Elizabeth thought about Liza and Bess.

Am I that mad? No, I don't hear voices like that.

Although Elizabeth's voices had argued over a year ago during a drinking binge, the altercation was brought on by extreme intoxication and had no bearing on what happened in reality. Her voices were part of herself.

She saw a man among the crowd across the street, watching the woman intently, a strange fascination in his gaze. He glanced up even as Elizabeth recognized him. The gentleman was the man she'd been seeking. She made her way toward him across the street, carefully avoiding contact with the madwoman.

"Elizabeth," the gentleman said.

How does he know my name?

You've seen him eyeing you, Bess said. *He's become so interested in you that he's asked around to find out your name.*

Bess's voice sounded foolishly hopeful. Elizabeth listened for her cynical voice.

No doubt you met him during one of your drunken spells and don't remember, Liza said.

That seemed more probable, though the suggestion held no charm at all. Short of believable, Bess's idea was more appealing.

"Hello," Elizabeth said to the gentleman, smiling brightly.

He pointed toward the woman acting like a fire engine and smirked.

"They threw her out of the tavern a while ago," Elizabeth said with a chuckle.

While he seemed somewhat familiar, she thought she would remember more clearly a gentleman of his appearance. He was a square-built man, old enough to be established but young enough—younger than her forty-five years—to have kept his looks. In his dark suit, overcoat, and billycock, he appeared to be a man of business, not a laborer.

Perhaps he knew Lettie. Had her twin become dissatisfied with her marriage and become involved with the man behind her husband's back?

Could be she has something going with the fellow that might help you, Liza said. *Take what you can and get out before things get ugly.*

Lettie is your deserving half, Bess said. *You won't feel good about taking from her.*

Lettie belongs to herself, Liza said. *She deserves nothing while you suffer. Play along with him and see what he has to offer.*

Liza's words were ugly, but excusable because Elizabeth didn't want to care about her twin.

"Let's get out of the crowd and have a drink," he said, taking her hand when she was close enough. His accent was odd, possibly American.

Elizabeth and the gentleman, who she could not help but think of as a client, hurried away from the crowd.

"You're a beauty tonight," he said as they walked, turning to her several times to take a look.

The rose has done me a lot of good, she thought as she smiled for him.

They hurried up Aldgate High Street and took the fork onto Commercial Road. Elizabeth glanced at him as they went, trying to figure out where she might have met him.

He had yet to say where they were going, and she was becoming winded. Finally she slowed and rested at the intersection with Church Lane.

"I'm going too fast," he said, turning back for her. "I'm sorry." He approached, took her in his arms, and kissed her mouth. He smelled good. His embrace was intimate and strong as he put his whole body into the effort. Elizabeth kissed him back with a passion partly driven by the hope that he was the man Jon had asked her to find.

When the gentleman stepped back, she asked, "Where shall we go?" Hopefully, he would suggest a place to eat and then feed her.

"The Bricklayer's Arms," he said. "Now, no more questions." Again, he kissed her, then hurried off up the road. She followed and he turned north at Settles Street. She caught up with him as he was entering the pub. They sat and had a simple meal of potatoes, bread and cheese. Elizabeth had nothing to drink. He had a glass of beer.

She tried to question him, to draw him out and learn who he was, but he deflected her questions for a while, then said, "No more!" He held up his hands as if fending her off. "I'll keep my secrets, and you keep yours. I prefer you a mystery. Please allow me to be the same for you."

He's hiding something, Liza said, *but then most men hide their true nature to get what they want. Just make sure to get something out of him in return.*

The gentleman had an imagination. Elizabeth liked that. He kept his eyes on her as they finished their meal. His expression and shifting gaze suggested that he thought she was fascinating. Although somewhat uncomfortable with the rapt attention, she was also flattered. Exiting the pub, they encountered falling rain. The gentleman laughed and turned her back toward the entrance. He pressed her against the wall gently, and kissed her again.

A man sitting near the exit within the establishment shouted through the open door, "Bring her back in and buy her a drink—buy us all a drink!" Elizabeth and her client ignored the man.

The fellow sitting next to the patron called out, "That's Leather Apron got his arms 'round you."

Elizabeth recognized that as one of the names the papers had given to the Whitechapel Murderer.

Could be that's what he's hiding, Liza said.

Nobody would bother to harm me, Elizabeth thought. *How would anyone find satisfaction in that?*

She laughed and ran out into the rain, heading back toward Commercial Road. The gentleman followed, and when he caught up with her, they continued together in the light downpour.

You only think that because you feel sorry for yourself, Liza said. *It's easy to think you're immune to danger when you don't value your own life and you believe you've gone unpunished for too long.*

Elizabeth knew what Liza referred to, and was tired of her sniping.

Crossing Commercial Road and moving west, they entered Back Church Lane where several of the lamps along the way were not lit and the gloom thickened. Her client's face was shadowed beneath his hat.

The risk is worthwhile, Elizabeth thought, then added defiantly, *and it's exciting too.*

The rain was intermittent as they moved south to Boyd Street and turned west. Again, the way was poorly lit.

Do you mean the risk is worth it, Liza asked, *even if you're not?*

Perhaps I have him fooled.

Or the other way round.

They turned north into Berner Street and paused to rest out of the wetness under the overhanging eve of a building. The gas lamps were all lit along the street—at least six of them—and more people were about. Seeing her client's smiling face more clearly reassured her. She was uncomfortable in her wet clothes, yet so thrilled with the attention of the gentleman that she didn't care. He took her in his arms and reached around to pet her backside.

"It's been a long time," she said.

"Do you mean since you felt the touch of a man?"

"Yes," she said, then she donned a sad expression. "I lost my husband when the Princess Alice went down."

"You're saying you haven't been touched in ten years?" He had a playful smile and she knew he'd seen through her lie.

Elizabeth didn't want to appear more lascivious than he wanted her to be. "Perhaps a little bit," she said, risking a coquettish smile.

"Ha!" he said, clearly pleased, "you would say anything but your prayers."

Elizabeth laughed. *Good*, she thought, *he's not prudish.*

She also didn't want to appear too eager. She broke from him gently and walked north and he went with her. They passed The Nelson public house at Fairclough Street, and heard singing coming from within.

Although near midnight, a greengrocer shop north of the pub was open and selling through its front window.

"The grapes look good," the gentleman said. "Which will you have, my dear, black or white?"

The fruit would give Elizabeth a stomach ache if she swallowed anything other than their juice. She craved the sweetness. "The black ones are plump," she said. "I'll have those."

"Half a pound, sir," he said to the shopkeeper.

The elderly fellow folded newspaper into a sack, placed a couple of black grape bunches in it, and passed the package through the window. Her client took the sack, paid the man, chose a few grapes for himself, and handed the rest to Elizabeth.

Holding the sack of grapes, she moved north on Berner Street and he followed.

The fruit is a delightful extravagance, Bess said. *This is a generous and imaginative fellow.*

Yes, Elizabeth thought. *Quite possibly, he already sees our time together as something more than a transaction.*

He's buying your affection, Liza said.

Elizabeth took a deep breath and pushed the cynical words from her mind. She put a grape in her mouth and crushed it lightly.

They had not walked far before the gentleman guided her toward the wall of a building. He pressed her against it lightly while kissing her, sharing the grape juice in his mouth and using his tongue to take the grape from her mouth. As they lingered in the light drizzle, embracing and kissing, Elizabeth tried to think of how to draw her client ever closer, to encourage him to treat her as a lover.

Abruptly, he pulled away. She was concerned until she saw his crooked smile.

"You hold here," he said. "I'll go to my room and be back in a trice with a bottle of fine, sweet wine."

"You could get a bottle at The Nelson," Elizabeth said. She placed another grape in her mouth.

"Not like the bottle I've got in my room."

Elizabeth didn't want him to get away. "I'll go with you."

He looked down, shaking his head slowly, and she knew he didn't want to be seen entering his home with a woman of her caliber. "It's not far," he said, looking up again. "I'll be right back with the sweetest wine you've ever tasted."

She couldn't anticipate whether her cynical voice wanted to keep the client or allow him to get away, and was surprised that Liza remained silent through the exchange.

The grapes were good, but to have the sweet nectar of the fruit with alcohol in it was a powerful temptation. She was inclined to risk temporary separation from her client to have some of the wine. She also needed to spit out the skin, seeds, and pulp of the grape in her mouth, and not wanting to be indelicate in his presence, she merely nodded her head, and he walked away.

28

TOMORROW'S EMBRACE

12:30 AM, September 30, 1888

Chilled from standing alone on Berner Street in the damp night for the last ten minutes, Elizabeth cursed herself silently, and decided that if her client didn't come back by the time she finished her grapes, she'd give up on him.

She ate the grapes slowly. Seven remained in the sack she held in her left hand. One stem of the fruit lay on the wet footway at her feet. As she wiped grape juice from her lips with one of her handkerchiefs, Elizabeth peered into the gloom, looking out for her gentleman among the people moving about the area. So close to midnight, the neighborhood was remarkably busy. Her vision wasn't what it had been when she was younger, and she saw most clearly near rather than far. Despite the numerous street lamps, people walking along the lane were almost upon her by the time she saw them. Accustomed to the risks of waiting on the street, however, she restrained her unease.

The dampness from the scattered rains was bringing out the ache in her old leg injury. Elizabeth bent and rubbed the unevenness of her right shin, where the bones had not been set correctly after her fall in the barn so long ago. She needed a drink to ease her aches and pains, and thought about going into The Nelson and trying to find a fellow to buy her one, but then she might miss her client. She could kick herself for not trying harder to get the gentleman's name.

There will be plenty of time for that, Bess assured her.

The words from her innocent voice were exactly what Elizabeth needed to hear. She welcomed the hopeful perspective.

He's worth the wait, Bess continued, *because he's a different sort. There's something special in his eyes, his manner, something that says he cares deeply about you. He's an educated gentleman, a fellow with taste and—*

—and most importantly, an income, Liza added. *It doesn't matter much what sort he is as long as he spends his money on you and you get away in the end.*

So, Liza did still have some enthusiasm for the gent.

The liaison will lead to a warm, clean bed and plenty to eat, Bess said.

With your luck, you won't get anything so grand, Liza said. *Although he might be something better, it doesn't take much to be superior to Mr. Kidney.*

She tries to take my courage away, Elizabeth thought, *just when I need it the most.* Increasingly, ever since she had promised herself that she'd always listen to the opinions of both her voices, Liza's black tongue had become particularly cruel, testing Elizabeth's resolve to keep the pledge.

You made that promise for your own protection, Liza said.

Protection indeed, Elizabeth thought. *At what cost? How many opportunities have your warnings kept me from enjoying over the years?*

How many dire straits might you have avoided by ignoring the child? Liza asked.

Elizabeth didn't want to know the answer to either question. What she wanted was distraction from her own thoughts.

She put a grape in her mouth and tore the peel off with her teeth and spat it out. She extracted the seeds and spit them out, then rolled the globular fruit pulp around with her tongue, slowly crushing it and extracting the sweet, delicious juice.

As she spit out the depleted pulp, she saw a young couple in quiet conversation pass through the open gates across the street beside the International Working Men's Educational Club, perhaps coming out from the tenement behind it. They moved slowly down the street, touching and laughing.

A man with a mustache and a small, peaked cap emerged out of the darkness to the south. Elizabeth was disappointed to see he wasn't her returning client.

Seeing her, the mustachioed man approached. "Do you want company?" he asked.

"No, not tonight," she said. Not wanting to miss an opportunity, though, she added, "Some other night."

He grumbled and backed away slowly, reluctantly, and stumbled off into the night toward the north. He was drunk.

You're better off with him gone, Liza said.

Still, if he'd made an offer, Elizabeth thought, *I should have gone with him.*

She had spent the six pence, earned working for Mrs. Tanner, earlier in the evening at the Hoop and Grapes pub. Elizabeth didn't have the price of a night's doss. She was fairly certain, however, that if she knocked up the deputy at the common lodging, the woman would let her in.

Elizabeth leaned against the brick building behind her and gave another glance up Berner Street toward the south, the direction her client had taken when he'd departed. She put another grape in her mouth and repeated the long process of taking it apart, swallowing the juice, and spitting out the rest.

Her attention was caught by a man she hadn't noticed before. He stood partly in shadow across the street, lighting his pipe.

She put another grape in her mouth as she watched him.

Since Bess had said favorable things about her client, Elizabeth would have to listen to what Liza had to say about him. Indeed, Elizabeth felt the cynical voice rising up. She knew Liza would likely insist that he wouldn't return. Then, assuming that he would come back, she'd say that he merely wanted to fornicate, and that he was just another adulterer who had no interest in her wellbeing.

But before Liza could have her say, Elizabeth's thoughts were interrupted as the mustachioed drunkard with the peaked cap returned.

"You're coming with me," he said, grabbing her left wrist and yanking her into the street. The sack of grapes hit granite paving stones and he inadvertently kicked it away into shadows.

"No," Elizabeth cried, twisting out of his grip. "No, no!"

She saw a bearded man walking up the lane behind the mustachioed man, and thought perhaps he'd help her. Instead, the bearded one moved to the other side of the road and continued on his way.

Elizabeth's assailant reached for her shoulders, held her for a brief moment, and looked her in the eyes.

He's drunk, Liza said. *Don't show fear.*

"You're no' such a fine Judy," he hissed, then spun Elizabeth around and shoved her down onto the damp footway.

She cried out in pain as her knees struck paving stones.

The drunkard turned and shouted something she couldn't make out, possibly to the man smoking the pipe in the shadows or to the bearded fellow. Both reacted as if threatened, and hurried away toward the south, while the drunkard disappeared into the night, back to the north.

Elizabeth had suffered worse from clients on other occasions.

As soon as the danger had passed, she was calm again. She couldn't see what had become of her bag of grapes. One piece of the fruit remained in her right hand, and she placed it in her mouth. As she got up and dusted herself off, something nagged at her—she knew she'd forgotten to do something of great personal importance. With increasing unease, she struggled to recollect. Whatever it was eluded her.

She backed up against the wall of the brick building behind her, straightened her clothing, and tried to adopt a dignified stance. Since she'd lost a couple of the grapes in the scuffle, she considered rescinding her promise to give up on her client upon finishing off her fruit.

As she rolled the pulp of her last grape around in her mouth, she realized what was bothering her: She hadn't listened to what Liza had to say about the gentleman. Again, the cynical voice rose up, but was interrupted before she could have her say.

Elizabeth's client appeared out of the gloom on the opposite side of the street, carrying an oblong package wrapped in newspaper. He had yet to see her. She quickly spit out the remains of her last grape.

Why would he wrap the wine in newspaper? Liza said. *This fellow is up to no good.*

I won't have it, Elizabeth thought. *Your black tongue will not dissuade me from taking up with this man.*

He waved to her as he approached.

He'll—Liza began.

"Enough!" Elizabeth said, cutting her off.

Startled, the gentleman stopped. He glanced to either side as if looking out for danger.

She repeated the word, "enough," as if she were coughing; as if that were the sound of her cough.

Silencing Liza was a serious breach of her promise to herself, but at the moment Elizabeth needed Bess's hope more than ever. She walked quickly across the street to meet the gentleman at the gates beside the International Working Men's Educational Club.

"I didn't mean to startle you," she said.

He had calmed quickly.

"For your cough, my dear," he said, offering her a small packet.

She could feel pills inside—cachous, perhaps.

They embraced and kissed, leaning back. The gate gave a little as they pressed against it. The gentleman pushed on the doorway and it opened further. "Let's go in for some privacy."

Elizabeth nodded enthusiastically and followed him through the opening into the darkness beyond. She heard a fumbling as if he'd stumbled, and felt him grab for her. She tried to steady him and he grabbed her by the neck and squeezed so hard Elizabeth felt her eyes bulge from their sockets. She clutched at his arms to break his grip, but they were as firm as the limbs of an oak. She tried to cry out, to gasp for air. Nothing flowed in either direction.

She looked toward her client's face, hoping he'd see that she was suffering and relent. His features were hidden in shadow. Elizabeth couldn't believe he meant to harm her. They were having such a good time together. Somehow, his grip was a mistake.

Blackness crept into the edges of her vision. She had finally reached the darkest bowels of the London beast, and as the darkness engulfed her, she knew that at least she wouldn't have to face what was to come.

Elizabeth lay on damp paving stones. Lightheaded, she found she couldn't rise. Her client had released her.

Elizabeth's neck felt strange. She placed the back of her hand to her throat and felt a warm flow. Pulling the hand away, she saw dark liquid on her knuckles. Even in the dim light, the droplets were red.

Elizabeth tried to cry out. The effort brought a pain in her throat.

No, I haven't been cut! Elizabeth screamed within. Panicked, her thoughts came in a rush, looking for a way out.

If the man had cut someone, that would be her twin.

The wound was meant for Lettie! The fellow belonged to her. I should be safe in bed at this hour. Let it be Lettie.

The silhouette of the man was poised above Elizabeth. Although she tried to picture Lettie beneath the shadowed figure with *her* throat cut, Elizabeth couldn't see Lettie suffer.

She's the better twin; a mother, not a prostitute. Lettie never harmed anyone.

Elizabeth couldn't wish such a cruel act upon her friend. No, she would accept the wound rather than that.

As the figure shifted beside her, the edge of a long blade in his hand reflected a dim orange light. The knife came closer. He became still as the sounds of a wagon and hooves on paving stones came from the street outside. The sounds ceased right outside the gate. The man, her client, the shadow, withdrew the knife, rose, and fled away from the gate, deeper into the yard.

The gash in her neck stung. The warm blood cooled quickly. A hollow grew in her head, in her thoughts, as the dark liquid ran away into the gloom.

You're merely weary, Bess said. *Rest until help comes.*

Where was Liza?

Gone, Elizabeth thought, *because my battles are over.* The thought was frightening. With each excited pulse, her heart dumped more of her life onto the pavement.

Again, Elizabeth tried to rise. One struggle—one with herself—remained unsettled.

Liza stirred—she had *not* fled.

Bess is right, she said as if fighting to speak, as if the wound were in *her* throat. *You're strong. You'll recover.*

Still, Elizabeth fought weakly to lift herself.

The old woman would have forgiven you, Liza said. *You gave her what she needed. You gave her—*

—*rest,* Elizabeth thought, and the word itself was calming. She ceased to fight, turned onto her left side, and gratefully closed her eyes.

Bess drew her into a comforting embrace.

The gash in Elizabeth's neck would heal and she'd resume her search for something better tomorrow.

Acknowledgments

Thanks to Cameron Pierce, Kisten Alene, Melody Kees Clark, Eric M. Witchey, Jill Bauman, Susan Stockell, Mark Edwards, Steven Savile, Mark Roland, Simon Clark, Charles Muir, Laurie Ewing McNichols, Ross E. Lockhart, and Pigg.

About the Author

Alan M. Clark grew up in Tennessee in a house full of human bones and old medical books. He has created illustrations for hundreds of books by authors such as Stephen King, Ray Bradbury, Joe R. Lansdale, and Brian Keene. Awards for his illustration work include the World Fantasy Award and four Chesley Awards. He is the author of thirteen books, including *Of Thimble and Threat: The Life of a Ripper Victim*, the western *The Door That Faced West*, the southern gothic *A Parliament of Crows* (Lazy Fascist Press, 2012) and *The Paint in My Blood*, a full-color collection of his artwork. Alan M. Clark and his wife, Melody, live in Oregon.

Visit him online at www.alanmclark.com.

CPSIA information can be obtained at www.ICGtesting.com
Printed in the USA
LVOW11s0218190316

479865LV00003B/151/P